MONSTERIOUS

THE SNATCHER OF RAVEN HOLLOW

MONSTERIOUS
THE SNATCHER OF RAVEN HOLLOW

MATT MCMANN

putnam

G. P. Putnam's Sons

G. P. PUTNAM'S SONS
An imprint of Penguin Random House LLC, New York

First published in the United States of America by G. P. Putnam's Sons,
an imprint of Penguin Random House LLC, 2023

G. P. Putnam's Sons is a registered trademark of Penguin Random House LLC.
Penguin Books & colophon are registered trademarks of Penguin Books Limited.

Visit us online at PenguinRandomHouse.com.

Library of Congress Cataloging-in-Publication Data is available.

Printed in the United States of America

ISBN 9780593530726 (hardcover)
ISBN 9780593530740 (paperback)
1st Printing

LSCC

Design by Nicole Rheingans
Text set in Maxime Pro

To Kilian and Kennedy,
my favorite Dungeon Masters

PROLOGUE

THE CREATURE slipped through the moonlit forest like a wraith.

Swiveling its shaggy head, it searched the thick foliage with glowing green eyes. When an imposing rock wall barred its path, the creature paused, peering into the gloom. At the base of the cliff stood a black opening like the mouth of a giant snake. Raising its beaklike muzzle, the creature sniffed the humid night air. Moments later, it stooped and entered the cave, moving easily through a dark, twisting passageway.

Rounding a final bend, it emerged into an expansive chamber. Silvery moonlight poured through a gap overhead, casting the creature's eerie shadow against a wall. Stalactites hung from the ceiling like giant stone bats. Pale crayfish darted through the chill water pooled in depressions in the floor. The creature ran a hand over a rough stone ledge, the scrape of its claws cutting the silence. It gazed around the chamber with a low growl of satisfaction.

Yes. This would do nicely.

CHAPTER 1

"HEY, CHECK that out," Teo said.

Logan looked down the sidewalk, squinting in the blinding summer sun. Outwardly, Logan and Teo were opposites—he was short and stocky, with blond surfer-boy hair and pale skin, while Teo was tall and willowy, with brown skin and short ink-black hair. They'd been best friends since the third grade, when she'd stopped Robby Thomas from sticking Logan's head through the monkey bars. Again.

"What is it?" he asked, shielding his eyes.

"I think it's a stroller," she said.

"How did a stroller end up on the side of the road?"

"Ooh, maybe there's a baby inside!"

Logan sighed. Teo always hoped for things to be more exciting than they actually were. In their small town of Raven Hollow, she was usually disappointed. "Right," he said. "I'm sure someone just abandoned their baby."

They walked over to the stroller.

It was empty.

"It probably fell off a truck when someone was moving," Logan said.

"Or maybe they threw it away on purpose," Teo said mysteriously.

"Why toss it? This looks almost new."

She chewed her lip. "I guess. Hey, there's a name on it—Dankworth." She scrunched up her nose as she pulled out her phone and began typing. "Sounds like the smell of a swampy-butt diaper." A few moments later, she looked up. "Got it."

"Got what?"

"An address. Only one Dankworth in town. It's not far. Maybe we should return this."

"But what about the pool?" Logan whined. It was sweltering, and he'd already put on sunscreen to keep from turning into Lobster Boy. Their plan to swim at the community center sounded a lot better than pushing a random stroller across town.

"Come on, Logan. It'll be an adventure."

He rolled his eyes. "What could possibly be adventurous about an empty stroller?"

CHAPTER 2

THE DANKWORTHS' house was small but well-kept, though the front lawn was overgrown and full of dandelions. Logan stayed with the stroller beside the porch steps while Teo knocked on the front door.

It opened abruptly. A young man with bags under his eyes and a short, ragged-looking beard stood in the doorway. "What do you want?" he demanded.

"Uh . . . um . . . Mr. Dankworth?" Teo said. Her normal confidence was shaken by the man's harsh tone. "We . . . uh . . . found your stroller and just wanted to bring it back."

He looked confused for a moment before glancing past her to where Logan stood with the stroller. Logan gave an awkward wave. Mr. Dankworth didn't look irritated anymore. He looked *angry*. Without another word, he slammed the door in Teo's face.

She raised an eyebrow at Logan.

"That was weird," he said.

She walked down the steps. "And super rude."

"Think we should leave it?"

"I *may* have picked up on an I-don't-want-it vibe."

"Observant of you."

The door opened again, and a young woman stepped onto the porch, closing the door softly behind her. She was pale and looked like she hadn't slept in a week. "I'm sorry, kids. My husband . . . he's having a difficult time. We both are."

The woman noticed the stroller.

Then she put her face in her hands and began to sob.

Teo looked at Logan, her eyes wide. He shifted uncomfortably. He never knew what to do when people cried, especially grown-ups.

"Are you . . . okay?" he asked, then winced. *Obviously not, Sherlock.*

"Sorry." The woman sniffed, wiping her face with her sleeve. "I didn't mean to fall apart on you. Been doing that a lot lately."

"Do you need help?" Teo asked tentatively.

Mrs. Dankworth's lip trembled, and Logan felt his stomach clench. He was afraid she was about to start crying again.

"You can't help," she said. "It's our baby . . . She was stolen."

CHAPTER 3

LOGAN STARED at Mrs. Dankworth in stunned confusion. "Stolen? What do you mean?"

"Our daughter, Ellie, was taken from our nursery," she said.

"That's *terrible*," Teo said. "But I'm sure the police will find her."

The woman shook her head. "They don't have any leads. No call for ransom. Nothing. She just vanished one night." Mrs. Dankworth glanced at the stroller, then looked quickly away. "The stroller was too painful a reminder."

"So that's why you left it on the side of the road?" Logan asked.

"It was rattling in the back of our van when I was driving, making me think of Ellie. I couldn't take it anymore, so I stopped and threw it out."

Teo hesitated before saying almost apologetically, "Technically, that's littering."

Logan cringed. Sometimes that girl just couldn't help herself.

Mrs. Dankworth gave Teo a long, blank stare. Finally, she climbed the porch steps and said, "Thanks for being thoughtful, but please, take it away."

"We're really sorry—" Logan began, but the woman closed the door behind her. As he stared at the house, a chill seeped into his stomach.

"Wow, that is seriously awful," Teo said.

"And strange. I mean, who steals a baby?"

"So what do we do with the stroller? It's too nice to trash it."

"My cousin Gabby is still a baby. Maybe my aunt Roslyn can use it."

Logan called his aunt, but she didn't need one and suggested they donate it to the thrift store. They walked to Crawly Street and left the stroller at the drop-off door behind the shop. Eager to escape the heat, they wandered inside, skimming used paperbacks and looking at peculiar paintings.

Teo caught Logan sniffing a book. One of her eyebrows arched so high it disappeared behind her bangs.

"What?" he asked. "I like the smell of old books."

She turned away, muttering, "You are so weird."

When they walked outside, Teo grabbed Logan's arm and pointed. In the store window was a flyer with the photo of a baby. The caption said the child was missing and pleaded for information.

"Sound familiar?" Teo asked.

"But the last name's not Dankworth," Logan said. "It's a different family. So there are *two* missing babies in town?" A shiver ran through him as he thought of his seven-year-old sister, Meg. Hardly a baby, but still . . . "What's going on?"

"I don't know," Teo said with a determined gleam in her eye. "But we're going to find out."

CHAPTER 4

THE CREATURE stretched its long arms and sat up, blinking sleepily. Shafts of sunlight streamed through a rift in the cave ceiling, filling the chamber with a soft golden glow. Turning its back to the light, the creature lay down again and shifted to a more comfortable position on the rocky floor.

A few feet away, a sharp cry rang out, then faded to a gurgling murmur. The creature did not stir. When the heat faded and the darkness came, it would rise.

That was its favorite time to hunt.

CHAPTER 5

TEO SAT at her bedroom desk with her laptop open, while Logan sprawled on a beanbag chair with his phone. They were scrolling through internet search results for "who steals babies?" They came across a news report on the missing babies in Raven Hollow, but it had very little information, quoting the police as saying, "The investigation is ongoing."

Teo read another article and snorted in disgust. "Did you know some women pretend to be pregnant, then steal babies just to keep their boyfriend or husband from leaving them? No offense, but you all aren't worth it."

"No argument from me," Logan said. "Looks like it sometimes happens with carjacking too. The thief doesn't realize there's a baby in the back seat."

"Most of the stories I'm seeing are about babies being taken from public places—parks, train stations, carnivals, that kind of thing."

"Yeah, and when it happens at a house, it's usually during the day by someone who befriended the parents so they can steal the baby. Talk about creepy." Logan tossed his phone onto Teo's bed. "I'm hungry. Let's raid your dad's snack cupboard."

When Teo didn't respond, he threw a pillow at her head.

She glared at him. "Can I *help* you?"

"Pay attention to me."

"Logan. We're talking about missing babies here. This is serious."

"Yeah, but come on, we're twelve. The police can handle this."

"Not according to Mrs. Dankworth. No leads, remember?"

He sighed. "Okay, but I can't search on an empty stomach."

"Fine. There's a bag of Doritos in the pantry."

Logan went to the kitchen and grabbed the chips. And an apple. And some cheese sticks. And a box of cookies.

Teo's eyes remained glued to her computer as Logan dumped the food onto her desk. On the screen was a picture of a white room with a row of babies in small, clear-sided beds.

"Looks like an alien abduction photo," Logan said. "Hey, maybe that's what happened. The kids were sucked up in a beam of light by Martians."

Teo gave him a disapproving look. "This isn't a joke."

"I know that," he said, his lips now stained with

Dorito dust. "Just trying to lighten the mood. So what's that photo?"

"It's a maternity ward. I read a story about a woman who stole a newborn from a hospital by posing as a nurse. Can you imagine giving birth and then having someone steal your baby?"

"I definitely can't imagine giving birth. And I don't want to, so no details. But yeah, losing your kid like that would be awful."

"There are more stories like this one. Apparently, it's happened a lot." She closed her laptop and stood. "I think we should check it out."

"Check whut owt?" Logan said with a cheese stick hanging from his mouth like a giraffe's tongue.

"Raven Hollow General."

Logan's cheesy tongue drooped. "You want to go to the hospital? And what, walk into the maternity ward and say, 'Hey, Doc, lost any babies lately?'"

"*No,*" she said in a frosty tone. "I'll be more subtle."

"You're about as subtle as an angry moose."

She crossed her arms. "Are you coming or not?"

Logan hesitated before blowing out a breath. When Teo got an idea in her head, she was like a shark on chum. "Fine. But then we hit the arcade. It's summer break. We're supposed to be having fun."

"Solving mysteries *is* fun."

"I guess. But remember, Nancy Drew—this is one case we are *not* gonna solve."

CHAPTER 6

"SO DO we just, like, walk in?" Logan asked, nervously eyeing the building entrance as they locked up their bikes.

He'd always found hospitals intimidating. They were filled with doctors in white coats, strange equipment, and lots of sick people. It gave him the creeps.

"Follow my lead," Teo said. "And try not to act too . . . Logany."

She strode to the door before he could think of a reply. Grumbling, he hurried after her.

The lobby was pleasantly cool, a welcome relief after the humid bike ride that left Logan's shirt damp with sweat. Miniature trees in large planters stood on the gleaming tile floor. Generic artwork lined the walls, and the sharp smell of cleaning solution hung in the air. A curved wood-paneled desk stood across from the entrance.

Teo marched confidently up to an older woman sitting behind the desk. She wore a purple vest with a large name tag that read ASK ME! I'M HELEN, YOUR FRIENDLY VOLUNTEER.

The woman looked up as they approached. "Hello, dears. How can I help?"

"Good morning, Helen," Teo said with a grin. "That vest really sets off your hair color."

"Well, thank you!" Helen replied, primping her auburn hair with one hand. "I had it done last week."

"Excellent choice of shade," Teo said. "You remind me of my aunt Sophia, and everyone thinks she's beautiful."

"Aren't you the sweetest thing," Helen said. "Are you here to see someone?"

"Aunt Sophia," Teo said. "She just had a baby. We're so excited to meet my new cousin!"

"That's lovely," Helen said. "What's your aunt's last name?"

"Martinez," Teo said.

Helen typed on a computer, then frowned. "That's odd. I don't see a patient by the name of Sophia Martinez."

Teo looked politely puzzled. "My mom's already been up to see her. She texted me this morning saying it was okay for us to stop by."

Helen hesitated a moment. "I'm sure it's fine for you to go up while I look into it. Take the elevators to the second floor. The maternity ward is on the right. Enjoy your visit!"

They thanked her and headed to a bank of elevators. Teo wore a smug expression.

"Okay, that look is annoying, but I gotta admit,

that was impressive," Logan said as he pushed the button for the second floor.

Teo shrugged. "Old people love me."

The elevator opened onto a bustling hallway. A nurse in blue scrubs hurried past while two more sat behind a high counter beneath a large whiteboard. A woman in a hospital gown walked slowly along clutching a tall silver pole on wheels. Hanging from the pole was a bag of clear liquid connected to a tube that was taped to the woman's arm.

"What do we do?" Logan whispered.

Teo paused, glancing around. Then she squared her shoulders and walked briskly past the nurses' station. Logan followed, trying to look casual, but he felt like frogs were using his stomach for a trampoline. He tensed, waiting for someone to yell at them.

No one did. They headed down the stark white hallway, passing several open doors. Inside the rooms were women lying on beds, accompanied by friends and family. Some of them looked happy, while others just seemed exhausted.

They came to a window. On the other side of the glass was a large room with a double row of babies in clear plastic bassinets. Several nurses were checking on the newborns. Logan thought his little sister, Meg, would freak out being here. She loved babies—he thought they were messy and boring.

"This looks like that photo from the article," Logan said, gazing around and wondering how someone could kidnap a baby.

A nurse with a brown buzz cut and stubble beard walked up to a door beside the window. He was huge, with biceps bigger than Logan's thighs. Grabbing the ID badge that hung around his neck, he held it to a sensor above the door handle. When an indicator light turned from red to green, he opened the door and went inside.

"Looks pretty secure," Logan whispered.

Teo stared intently through the window, her eyebrows pulled down in a V shape.

The nurse walked to the end of a row, then rolled a crib back to the door. After exiting the nursery, he wheeled the baby down the hall and entered a room. Jerking her head for Logan to follow, Teo hurried after him.

Peeking through the door, they saw a woman sitting on a bed. As the nurse chatted with her, he scanned an ID band on her wrist, then scanned a similar band on the baby's arm. He nodded to her with a smile and turned to leave. Logan and Teo scrambled away from the door. She leaned casually against the wall while he pretended to be fascinated by a painting of a stuffed bear holding a yellow balloon.

Emerging from the room, the nurse noticed them and paused. "Are you two waiting to go in?"

"Us?" Logan said, looking at him in feigned surprise. "Uh . . . nope. We're all good, thanks."

"We're waiting for our aunt," Teo said. "I mean my aunt. We're not related. Obviously. We're together. I mean, not *together*, like romantically or anything. We're just . . . friends."

She swallowed hard, and a bead of sweat appeared on her forehead.

"Wow," Logan muttered, looking at the floor.

The nurse stepped closer. The *o* on his C. BOGDAN name tag was covered by a yellow smiley face sticker. It did not match his expression as he glared down at them.

"Are you two supposed to be here?"

CHAPTER 7

"UM . . . I mean . . . well, technically," Logan stammered, "you could say that we're . . . um . . ."

"We're investigating the baby kidnappings," Teo said firmly, looking the man in the eye. "We read that newborns are sometimes stolen from hospital nurseries, and we wanted to check it out."

She sure got her confidence back in a hurry, Logan thought. If he hadn't been so nervous, he would have laughed at seeing her stand up to the giant man, like a badger squaring off with a grizzly.

The nurse frowned. "Look, I'm going to have to ask—"

"Is there a problem here?"

A woman in a white lab coat with a stethoscope draped around her neck stopped beside the man. With her hair in a harsh bob and her severe expression, she was more intimidating than the linebacker nurse, Logan thought.

"I noticed these two hanging around, Dr. Patel," the nurse said. "They're investigating the disappearing infants and read that kidnappings sometimes happen in hospital nurseries."

The doctor blew a sharp breath from her nose like a flameless dragon. "Cases of child abduction from hospitals are very rare, and the majority are from many years ago. Hospitals like ours have long since implemented security measures like barcoded ID bands that make abductions nearly impossible today." She glanced at the nurse and said, "Show them out, Chad," before striding away.

Heads down, Logan and Teo walked to the exit, closely followed by the nurse. As they waited for an elevator, Logan said, "We're really sorry. We didn't mean any trouble."

The man's expression softened slightly. "It's okay. Sounds like you meant well, but Doc's right—it's more likely for a baby to be taken by Muma Pădurii than kidnapped from a maternity ward."

Teo looked up sharply. "Muma Pădurii? What's that?"

The man smiled. "Just a story my grandma used to tell me about an old forest crone who stole children. Scared me to death as a kid. My grandma's from Romania and believes a lot of the old folktales."

"She sounds pretty interesting," Logan said.

"Grandma Elena is definitely that," he said with a chuckle. "She keeps them entertained at the nursing home. Sometimes I run next door to visit during my lunch break."

The elevator dinged, and the door slid open.

He ushered them inside and said, "Now, stay out of trouble, you two."

Logan nodded and forced a smile.

Obviously, the man didn't know Teo.

CHAPTER 8

THE HEAT hit them like a hammer as they exited the lobby. Teo closed her eyes and soaked it in. After the chill of the hospital, it was a pleasant change—for about ten seconds.

"That Muma Pădurii sounded pretty scary," she said.

"Not as scary as that doctor. I thought *she* was going to eat us. Your power to charm adults is slipping."

"They weren't old enough," Teo said. "I need the geriatric factor."

"I think we can safely check this place off the kidnapping list," Logan said. "Security's pretty tight. Ready to hit the arcade?"

Teo didn't respond. She gazed past him with a faraway expression.

"I know that look," Logan said. "It usually comes right before we get in trouble."

"I was just thinking that while we're here, we might as well make another stop."

"Another stop? Where?"

Teo pointed to a large brick building across the street. The sign out front read SHADY ACRES NURSING HOME.

"You're joking," he said. "You want to visit Godzilla Nurse's grandma?"

"Why not? You said she sounded interesting."

"Anyone who can tell a good story is interesting, but I don't see the point."

Teo glanced away and shifted her feet. "I want to follow up on the lead."

Logan's face crinkled in confusion. "Lead? What lead?" Then he groaned. "Not that Muma whatever creature?"

"He said it steals children. There's a connection."

"It's a *story*, Teo. A myth. A legend. A folktale. And—minor point—we're not in Romania!"

"Yeah, but remember what Ms. Chéng told us in world history? Different countries have similar myths, and most of them have a basis in fact. We can at least ask his grandma to tell us the story. Besides, we'll make an old lady happy. What's the harm?"

Logan sighed. Arguing with Teo felt like playing tennis against a wall—no matter how good your shot, it always came back.

"I don't know . . ." he said.

"We'll do this, then hit the arcade," Teo cajoled. "I'll even give you five bucks in tokens."

Logan still thought it was a waste of time, but five bucks was five bucks. "Deal."

They crossed the street and entered the nursing home. In contrast to the clinical, sterile hospital, the lobby felt welcoming and comfortable, with brick walls, cushy chairs, and a bubbling fountain. Behind the front desk sat a Black girl in her late teens with white-rimmed glasses, and her hair stylishly gathered into two puffs. "Welcome to Shady Acres!" she said with genuine enthusiasm. "I'm Jasmine. Visiting today?"

"Uh . . . yeah," Logan said. "Is . . ." His eyes went wide as he realized they didn't know Grandma Elena's last name. Then he remembered the nurse's smiley-face ID tag. "Is Elena Bogdan available?"

"I love Elena!" Jasmine said. "She's so sweet. How do you know her?"

Logan shifted nervously. "Well, actually, we—"

"We're friends with her grandson from the hospital," Teo interrupted smoothly.

"Oh, Chad!" Jasmine said. "He's a nice guy. Not

many young people visit their grandparents in here, you know? Sign in and put on a visitor sticker, then I'll take you back."

After writing their names on a clipboard, they followed Jasmine down a wide hallway. This part of the building was similar to the hospital, only more homey. Skylights softened the harshness of the fluorescent bulbs, and oil-painted landscapes hung on the pale blue walls. Jasmine greeted people by name as they ambled slowly along using walkers or gripping handrails.

The group turned into a large rectangular room with a high ceiling. Residents sat at tables playing chess, doing crafts, or working on puzzles. Others sat on couches in front of a television. The far wall was lined with floor-to-ceiling windows overlooking a park with a path that wound beneath mature trees. Teo noticed a grassy, minty smell along with hints of butterscotch.

"Old-people smell," Logan whispered.

"It's nice," Teo whispered back.

Jasmine led them to an older white woman with silver hair sitting in a rocking chair. A colorful quilt rested on her lap. Eyes closed, her face was angled to catch the sunlight streaming through the window.

"Hi, Elena," Jasmine said. "Look who's come to visit you!"

Elena's eyes fluttered open with a smile. She gazed at Logan and Teo serenely for a moment. Then her face fell, and her mouth set in a firm line.

"I don't know *either* of you."

CHAPTER 9

LOGAN'S EYES went wide at Elena's sudden change. "I . . . um . . ."

"They said they were friends of Chad's," Jasmine said, looking at Teo and Logan with a puzzled expression.

Elena's face brightened, and she asked in a slight Romanian accent, "You know my Chad? So we haven't met before?"

"No, ma'am," Teo said. "Chad spoke so highly of you that we thought we'd stop by for a visit."

"Are you okay with this, Elena?" Jasmine asked. "I can have them leave if you're uncomfortable."

"Oh, no need for that, dear," Elena said.

Jasmine smiled. "I'll leave you to get acquainted, then."

As she walked away, Elena said, "Forgive me for being a bit harsh, kids. The only visitors I get are friends and family. When I didn't recognize you, I was afraid my mind was going. I know it will happen sometime, but to be honest, it frightens me."

"We understand," Teo said. "I'm sorry we showed up unannounced like this."

"Not at all," Elena said. "So how do you know Chad?"

"We met him when we were visiting the hospital," Logan said.

"He's a good boy," Elena said. "Always makes time to visit me. Now, what can I do for you?"

Teo sat on a nearby footstool and leaned forward.

"We were hoping you could tell us about Muma Pădurii."

Elena looked surprised. "Really? Whatever for?"

I'm wondering the same thing, Logan thought, but he bit his tongue. This was Teo's show.

"Some babies have been kidnapped recently," Teo said, "and we're trying to find out why."

Elena's face darkened. "Oh, yes. I heard about that on the evening news. Those poor parents."

Teo shifted her stool closer to the old woman. "Chad said you told him that Muma Pădurii stole children. We thought it was an interesting connection."

"But we know it's only a story," Logan added. He didn't want the woman thinking *their* minds were going.

Elena gazed at him with a thoughtful expression. "You sound like Chad. He only believes in what science can prove. Science is a wonderful thing, but it's not the only way to discover what's real."

"Are you saying there's some truth to the story of Muma Pădurii?" Teo asked.

"Perhaps," Elena said. "Not everything, of course. The stories have grown over time."

"What stories?" Logan asked, becoming intrigued in spite of himself.

Elena settled back in her chair and rested her frail-looking hands on her quilt. "Muma Pădurii is an ancient creature of the deep forest, a mother of trees. She normally hides from humans and is rarely seen, even when she's on the hunt."

"On the hunt for what?" Logan asked.

"Human flesh."

Story or not, he shivered.

"What does she look like?" Teo asked.

"She's a frightening thing," Elena said. "Tall with withered legs, her hair drooping to the ground like vines. Her skin is said to be like the bark of a tree, making her difficult to spot in the woods. She's heard more often than seen. I remember moans and shrieks coming from the Hoia Forest when I was a little girl in Romania." She trembled slightly. "Terrifying sounds."

"Did you ever see her?" Logan asked.

"No, and I'm glad of it," Elena said. "But my sister Daciana did, God rest her soul. She was hiking in the Hoia and noticed a campfire through the trees at twilight. She moved closer, and there was Muma Pădurii, ancient and terrible, hunched over the flames. Daciana said she'd never run so fast in her life."

They were silent for a few moments, all lost in their own thoughts.

"How does this creature steal babies?" Teo asked.

"She's clever," Elena said, "and has ways of luring unsuspecting people into the forest, where she captures and eats them. She's even been known to take children from their homes at night."

Teo gave Logan a knowing look. He shifted uncomfortably.

"But even if Muma Pădurii is real, she lives in Romania," Logan said. "She couldn't have anything to do with the missing babies here."

Elena shrugged. "True. And not true. Many countries have tales of a 'woman of the woods' like Muma Pădurii, but called by different names. And while she is a physical creature, she's also a spirit. She is found wherever her people are gathered." She eyed both children meaningfully. "Did you know there is a large population of Romanian immigrants in this area?"

Logan swallowed a lump in his throat.

"So how could you stop Muma Pădurii, or something like her, from stealing children?" Teo asked.

"She hates metal," Elena said. "As a mother of trees, and being treelike herself, she fears anything that can cut wood. Since she's also a spirit, she can be bound by protection spells. Speaking a protection spell over metal objects, then placing them in the woods at the four compass points, will create a barrier that Muma Pădurii cannot cross. But this must be done at night, when she stalks the forest."

Logan felt like a bowling ball landed on his stomach as Teo leaned forward, an intense gleam in her eyes. He already knew what she was going to ask.

"Can you teach us that protection spell?"

CHAPTER 10

AS THE sun dipped low behind the thick canopy of the forest, the creature stood at the mouth of the cave. Raising its shaggy head, it sniffed the still air while unconsciously flexing its claws. A growl that was almost a purr rumbled in its chest. The surrounding woods grew silent, as if the animals knew there was something nearby that didn't belong.

The creature glanced over its shoulder, listening. Then it slipped out and disappeared into the deepening gloom.

CHAPTER 11

LOGAN STARED at the odd collection of items on his mom's garage workbench—a broken pair of gardening clippers, a rusted spring, an old gear, and a long gray nail.

"Are you sure about this?" Logan asked.

"No," Teo admitted. "But Elena said anything would work as long as it's metal."

"You realize this whole thing is ridiculous, right?" Logan asked.

Teo shrugged. "Probably, but who knows?" Then she grinned. "Either way, it's kind of cool."

Logan didn't respond. He wished they'd stayed longer at the arcade. But he knew from experience it was best to let Teo get this latest obsession—the missing babies—out of her system. Then they could go back to a *real* summer of swimming, Castle Dread graphic novels, Moo Magic ice cream, and video games.

"Now we need to speak the protection spell over each item," Teo said.

She opened a note-taking app on her phone and propped it against a hunk of wood on the workbench. Picking up the nail, she held her other hand over it, hovering about an inch away. Reading from her phone, she chanted:

> *Muma Pădurii, creature of fury,*
> *By these words I stand.*
> *Come thorn and nettle, and by this metal,*
> *From this place be banned!*

They stared at the nail.

After a few moments, Logan said, "Looks the same."

Teo frowned slightly. "Well, yeah. The spell can work even if the nail doesn't glow or anything." Despite her positive spin, she couldn't quite hide the disappointment in her voice.

She repeated the spell over the other three objects before dropping them into her backpack. Hopping on their bikes, they headed down the street. The setting sun threw their elongated shadows ahead of them. Logan held up one hand, and the outline of his extended fingers looked like talons. He wondered if Muma Pădurii had claws, then tried to push that thought from his mind.

At the edge of town, they left the road and took a dirt track through the meadow to the woods. They got off their bikes, and Teo checked the GPS app on her phone.

"Due east is that way," she said, pointing into the forest.

The sun had set, and shadows were thick beneath the trees. "We could walk along the edge of the woods and leave the metal piece in the meadow," Logan said, trying unsuccessfully to sound casual.

"Elena said it needs to be in the forest where Muma Pădurii lives," Teo said, raising an eyebrow at him. "You can wait here if you're scared."

"Why should I be scared of a story? Lead the way."

Teo made no reply, but Logan guessed she noticed that he didn't actually deny being afraid.

As they entered the gloomy forest, rustling sounds came from the undergrowth. Logan knew it was probably just squirrels and rabbits, but not being able to spot them made him uneasy.

"This looks right," Teo said after checking her phone. She pulled the garden clippers from her pack and stuck them point first into the soft bark of a fallen tree. "One down, three to go."

They returned to their bikes and rode through downtown. The wonderful aroma drifting from

Mamma Gianni's Pizzeria set Logan's stomach growling.

At the bridge that marked the town's northern boundary, they laid their bikes on the riverbank and walked downstream, trying to avoid the mud. Ahead of Logan in the deepening twilight, Teo's head and shoulders were silhouetted against the glow of her GPS app.

After rounding a bend in the river, they came to a rocky outcropping. While Logan soaked in the cool breeze coming off the water, Teo climbed to where a large flat rock lay like a sacrificial altar. She pulled out the metal gear and placed it almost reverently on the stone. Logan thought the gear's perfectly symmetrical teeth looked out of place in this wild spot. He could almost imagine that they were completely isolated, far from the comfort and safety of civilization.

"Let's keep moving," he said, nervously eyeing the forbidding wall of dark trees beside them.

As they turned to head back, a strange shape at the edge of the woods caught Logan's eye. He froze.

Bathed in the soft light of the rising moon stood a tall figure. Draping tendrils of hair snaked down past withered legs. Barklike skin was splotched with patches of deep green moss. Huge, crooked claws reached out, ready to claim them.

Muma Pădurii had come.

CHAPTER 12

LOGAN'S HEART thundered in his chest while his throat clenched, choking off his scream.

He tried to run, but his feet seemed to be trapped in quicksand. A whimpering groan escaped his lips. He squeezed his eyes shut and raised his arms as a useless shield, waiting for Muma Pădurii's claws to pierce his skin.

"What are you doing?" Teo asked.

Logan slowly opened his eyes.

Teo stared at him with an expression of puzzled

amusement. Logan looked quickly past her to Muma Pădurii.

As the moonlight shifted, the creature vanished. In her place stood a tree. A tall, weathered tree, its heavy bark spotted with moss. Vines drooped along the trunk behind a pair of dead branches that pointed like arms toward the river.

"I . . . uh . . . nothing," Logan stammered. Unable to meet Teo's gaze, he glanced down to find his feet had sunk into the riverbank's deep mud.

Teo stared at him, then turned and spied the tree. A moment later, she gave a delighted cackle.

"You . . . you thought that was . . ." She doubled over with laughter, and soon tears were streaming down her face.

"Go ahead," Logan said. "Get it out of your system."

"And you call *me* gullible," she said, wiping her cheeks. "Wow. Thanks for that."

"Yeah, yeah, glad I could entertain you," he grumbled, grateful the darkness hid the flush in his cheeks.

She helped Logan pull free of the mud. Soon they were back on their bikes riding west, the neon-colored lights on Teo's wheels spinning hypnotically.

When they reached the western edge of town, the sky was like a pool of ink dotted with stars. They stopped their bikes under a streetlight and gazed at the murky woods. It felt like they were on an island, about to plunge into a dark ocean where unseen predators lurked.

Teo pulled two flashlights from her backpack and handed one to Logan. He reluctantly followed her through the tall pokeweed to the edge of the forest. Guided by her GPS app, they slipped into the trees accompanied by a choir of chirping crickets. The air felt sticky as they stumbled through the thick underbrush.

Finally, scratched and sweating, they pushed into

a small clearing filled with wildflowers. The high-pitched whine of mosquitoes sang in Logan's ears, and he swatted at them irritably.

"This will do," Teo said, reaching into her pack. She laid the rusted spring in a patch of bloodroot, the flowers' delicate white petals glowing in the moonlight. "Only one more to—"

A piercing scream shredded the night like tissue paper. Logan nearly jumped out of his mud-caked shoes.

"Please tell me that was my imagination again," he whispered.

Teo didn't answer. Her eyes were like twin moons, and her skin turned ashen.

Another shriek ripped through the darkness. Whatever bravado Logan had left shriveled like a leaf in a flame. Teo didn't know what could make such a hideous sound.

But it was coming closer.

Without a word, they bolted from the clearing, flying heedlessly through the thickets. Their flashlight beams jolted wildly as they ducked and dodged their way through the menacing woods. The scream came again, propelling them to even greater speed.

Logan and Teo burst from the trees and sprinted to where their bikes lay in a streetlamp's welcoming pool of light. They jumped on and tore away, pedaling furiously.

A final haunting wail echoed after them.

CHAPTER 13

THE CREATURE stood at the edge of the moon-lit clearing.

As the cries died away, it slid through the tangle of milkweed and bloodroot, heading toward the trees on the far side. Halfway across, the creature paused. A rusted spring lay at its feet. The monster's lip curled into a menacing snarl, revealing wicked-looking fangs.

Slowly, it raised its head and glared in the direction the humans had gone.

CHAPTER 14

THE NEXT morning, Teo and Logan huddled in a corner of the Hob, a hangout area reserved for teens in their local library. They were only twelve but figured that was close enough.

"How'd you sleep?" Teo asked, picking at a Band-Aid on her arm. They both had cuts and scrapes from last night's panicked flight.

Afraid she'd make fun of him, Logan considered lying, but the haunted look in her eyes changed his mind. "Not good. You?"

Teo shook her head. "Those screams. They didn't sound . . . human."

"Maybe they weren't."

Teo looked at him quizzically. "Are you saying it was Muma Pădurii?"

"Not her. When I couldn't sleep last night, I did some research. I think we might have heard a bobcat."

Teo's face scrunched in surprise. "Really? But it was so loud and . . . spooky."

"I watched some bobcat videos on YouTube. They sounded pretty similar."

"Oh," Teo said, managing to look both relieved and disappointed at the same time. "That's good, I guess. I mean, I'm glad we weren't almost killed by a monster."

Logan eyed her. "But you're kind of bummed there isn't one running around town?"

Her face broke into a sheepish grin. "Guilty."

"So can we forget about this Muma Pădurii stuff now?"

Teo chewed her lip. "I'll admit we didn't find her last night. And I know it's probably only a story. But I kind of want to finish the ritual, you know? Just in case."

Logan started to object but stopped himself when he caught her hopeful expression. If it was important to her, he was willing to tag along. That's what best friends did.

"Fine," he said. "But then I'm out, okay? No more woods."

Teo grinned. "Wanna head to your house with our haul?" She held up the stack of books they'd collected.

Logan sighed. "Aunt Roslyn has a doctor's appointment, so I said I'd babysit Gabby. My dad's dropping Meg off there too. She can't get enough of that kid." He looked thoughtful for a moment. "Hey, you could come with me."

Teo raised an eyebrow. "And why would I help you babysit?"

Logan tilted his head to one side, then smiled and blinked his eyes. "Because I'm adorable?"

"Try again."

He blew out a breath. "Okay, I'll split the money with you."

"Hmmm," Teo said. "Is lunch included?"

"I'll make the peanut butter and pickle sandwiches myself."

"Ew. I'll just take the cash."

CHAPTER 15

"SHE'S GOT my hair!" Meg squealed in delight.

She was on her knees leaning over Gabby, who was nestled in her bouncy seat on Aunt Roslyn's living room floor. Logan and Teo watched from the couch as Gabby clutched one of Meg's blond pigtails in her chubby fist.

"Careful, Meg," Logan said. "She's only six months old."

"I *am* being careful," Meg said, making a face at her big brother. "I know how to play with babies. My friend Ollie has one."

Teo stood up. "I'm gonna make lunch."

"I can do that," Logan said.

"No offense, but I've seen your culinary skills."

"I'll help!" Meg said. She ran to Teo, who bent down so Meg could climb on her back, and the two headed into the kitchen.

Logan moved to lie on his stomach next to Gabby, who gurgled and waved her arms like miniature windmills. He put his lips on her stomach and blew a raspberry. Gabby giggled in delight. He thought that was one of the coolest sounds in the world.

After lunch, Logan tried not to gag as he changed Gabby's diaper. He didn't think she was so cute anymore. He'd just put her down for a nap when Aunt Roslyn returned. She gave him some money, and soon they were walking to Logan's house.

Wordlessly, Teo held out her hand, and Logan gave her half the cash.

"Hey, what about me?" Meg protested.

"Forget it," he said. "We did all the work, remember?"

On reaching the house, Teo and Logan took their stack of library books to Logan's room and spent the rest of the afternoon reading. He flipped through a book on the US women's soccer team, while Teo buried herself in the latest in The Forgotten Five supernatural series.

Logan's mom appeared in the doorway. "We're leaving to drop off Meg. She's going camping with Lily's family for a week, remember?"

Logan thrust his arm in the air. "Yes!"

His mom smirked. "Okay, tone it down. Dad and I are going out afterward, so we left pizza money on the counter. Have fun."

An hour later, Logan and Teo gorged on Mamma Gianni's Hawaiian Pig Pie while bingeing episodes of *Mystery Hunters*. As the sun began to set, they climbed on their bikes and rode south past Mr. Abadi's horse stables. The normally docile animals neighed and shuffled nervously. Logan tried to convince himself that wasn't a bad sign.

There were fewer houses in the southern part of town, and when the pavement ended, so did the streetlights. Twilight had fallen, so they bumped along the dirt road with their flashlights held out like makeshift headlamps.

The road stopped at the woods. The evening breeze carried the stink of manure from nearby farms.

"Gotta love that fresh country air," Logan said.

"Kinda smells like your room," Teo replied.

"Hey, I'm doing this for you, remember?"

"We're doing it for the babies."

"Whatever." Logan glanced skyward. Heavy clouds smothered the stars, and his skin prickled, warning of a coming storm. *Terrific.*

Following Teo's app, they trudged into the dark woods. The trees creaked ominously in the rising wind. Beyond that, it was eerily quiet. Logan reminded himself that last night's "sighting" was only a spooky tree, and the screams were probably just a bobcat. That almost proved there was no terrifying monster out here ready to eat them. While his brain applauded that logic, the rest of him was unimpressed.

"How much farther?" Logan asked, his heart rate steadily climbing.

Teo checked her phone, then gestured toward a mound ahead of them. "Up there should work."

As they crested the low rise, Teo pulled off her backpack and retrieved the nail. Logan tripped on a root and went down hard, banging his knee on a rock.

"Urgh!" he said loudly. "I'm really getting sick of—"

"Shhh!" Teo hissed and put her hand on his shoulder. Wordlessly, she pointed.

Below them in a small clearing was a campfire, its flickering light making shadows dance on the trees. Beside the fire crouched a figure, its sharp silhouette black against the flames. Logan thought it was a strange place for camping. He looked around for a tent or other equipment but saw none.

Then Elena's words came back to him. She'd said her sister once saw Muma Pădurii in the woods, hunched over a campfire. Despite the warm summer night, an icy chill trickled down his spine. Beside him, Teo tensed.

A flash of lightning split the sky, and for an instant, the woods blazed with light.

Logan gasped. The figure was an old woman wrapped in a ragged shawl, her long, stringy hair dangling past her shoulders. Moments later came a boom of thunder, and Logan's heart nearly shattered his rib cage. The old woman turned and pierced them with her gaze, her eyes glinting strangely in the firelight.

Quick as a snake, Teo knelt and jammed the long nail into the earth.

Then they fled like they were being chased by something far worse than a storm.

CHAPTER 16

"I'M GLAD I got home before my parents did,"
Logan said to Teo. "I didn't have to explain why I was
drenched."

The storm had blown itself out overnight, leaving
a fresh, clean scent in the late-morning air. Logan
sprawled on the beanbag chair in Teo's room while
she lay on her bed propped up on her elbows.

"Lucky you. I got lectured about riding my bike at
night in a thunderstorm."

"Ouch," he said with a sympathetic grimace. "Any more thoughts on that lady in the woods?"

"After the spooky tree and the bobcat, I'm trying to be realistic. I mean, it was probably just a woman camping. But you gotta admit, it was a crazy coincidence."

Logan reached out and absentmindedly scratched Bently, Teo's big lump of a bulldog, whose massive head rested on his leg. "Yeah, she looked human. Maybe she doesn't have a home or just likes being alone in the woods."

"At least we completed the ritual," Teo said.

"Excellent. I'm ready to have my summer back. Up for a swim?"

They spent the afternoon at the community pool, then hit Moo Magic, their favorite ice cream shop. In the evening, they had a cornhole tournament with Logan's parents, and his mom grilled burgers. The fact that Meg was gone camping made it even sweeter.

For Logan, the rest of the week flowed by in a leisurely stream of contentment, interrupted by occasional chores assigned by his parents. Teo felt flat and restless now that there was nothing more to do on the baby-snatching mystery.

Logan's Sunday afternoon Zen mode cracked when he heard the front door slam and a singsong voice call out, "I'm home!"

Ugh. Meg. It was good while it lasted.

While Meg rattled on about her camping adventures, Logan's dad made spaghetti for dinner, then they had a family game night. They played Parcheesi, Logan's favorite, and he got to be the elephants.

The next day, Logan was playing fetch with Bently in Teo's backyard. She'd gone inside to get them lemonade ten minutes ago. The afternoon sun made him feel like a baked potato, and he was irritated at the delay. When the back door finally opened, Teo walked toward him, curiously empty-handed.

"Hey, what about the . . ." he began, then paused when he noticed her strained expression. "You okay?"

She held up her phone.

"News just broke. Another baby was taken last night."

CHAPTER 17

BENTLY DROPPED the slobbery ball at Logan's feet. When he didn't pick it up, she bumped her head against his leg.

"The ritual," Teo said. "It didn't work."

Logan blew out a breath. "We knew the whole Muma Pădurii thing was probably just a story. I feel awful for that family, but it's not a surprise that leaving junk in the woods didn't stop the kidnappings."

Teo bit her lip. "Maybe . . . maybe we did it wrong."

"Don't go there," he said, frustration creeping into

his voice. "We did everything Elena told us. I know you. You really want there to be something supernatural about this town, but face it, Teo—there isn't. We're just boring old Raven Hollow."

She ran her toes slowly through the grass. "I guess."

"Good. Now, how about that lemonade?"

Teo hesitated. "I think we should talk to her."

"Who do you need to talk to about lemonade?"

She threw him an exasperated look. "Elena. I think we should ask her why the ritual didn't work."

Logan's eyes went wide. "Because it's made-up! There *is* no Muma Pădurii!"

Teo's mouth set in a firm line, and she squared her shoulders. "I'm going. Right now. See you later." She turned and marched into the house.

Logan laced his fingers on top of his head with a sigh. Bently bumped his leg again and looked up expectantly.

"Sorry, girl," he said. "I've gotta go see an old lady."

Logan caught up to Teo in the garage as she was putting on her bike helmet. She gave him a cool look.

"You still owe me a lemonade," he muttered as he climbed on his bike.

Teo cracked a smile. "Dork."

"Bonehead."

Fifteen minutes later, they locked their bikes to the rack outside Shady Acres. Jasmine waved enthusiastically when they entered the lobby. "Elena's at lunch, but she's almost done. You can wait in her room if you want. Down the hall, room 118."

Elena's room was simple but cozy. A bookcase stood against one wall, filled with novels, puzzles, and a collection of miniature owl statues. In addition to the bed, there was a comfy chair by a window overlooking the park. A familiar-looking quilt lay on the seat.

Logan walked to a painting hanging near the bed. It depicted a stream running through a forest of strangely curved trees. A small brass plaque on the bottom of the frame read:

MEMORIES OF ROMANIA: THE HOIA FOREST

BY ELENA BOGDAN

"Elena painted this," he said.

Teo came over. "It's really good. And wasn't the Hoia Forest where her sister saw Muma Pădurii?"

"It was," said a soft voice.

They turned to see Elena leaning on a polished wooden cane in the doorway, a smile on her face. "It's nice of you kids to visit again."

"Our pleasure," said Teo.

"You're a really good artist," Logan said.

"You are kind." Elena walked over and settled into the chair with a contented sigh. "I spent much of my childhood playing in that forest. It could be eerie at times, but I loved it. When I close my eyes, I can still catch the wildflowers' scent and hear the whisper of the trees." For a moment, her face took on a dreamy expression. Then she stirred and looked at them. "But you didn't come to hear an old woman reminisce. How can I help?"

Teo sat on a footstool facing Elena. There were no other chairs, so Logan perched on the edge of the bed.

"It's about the ritual," Teo said. "We thought we did everything right, but another baby was stolen last night."

Elena sighed deeply. "I am sorry to hear that, but not completely surprised. I'm sure you did fine with the ritual, dears. Muma Pădurii is very old and very clever. She has learned many ways to overcome attempts to keep her from hunting." She gazed at them sympathetically. "The aliens had the same problem."

Logan looked up sharply. When he glanced at Teo, her face mirrored his confusion.

"Um . . . I'm sorry," he said carefully. "Did you say 'aliens'?"

She nodded soberly. "Yes. They were interested in Muma Pădurii too. The ritual didn't work for them either. But they still like to listen to my stories whenever they take me."

"Take you?" Teo asked weakly.

"The little scamps," Elena said with a smile. "They come at night while everyone is sleeping. They're shy, you know, but friendly. Always get me back in time for breakfast. I do love a toasted English muffin with jam."

Teo and Logan stared at each other. She swallowed hard. He had a queasy feeling.

"Well . . . um . . . okay, thanks, Elena," Teo said as she stood up. "We have to go now."

"Yeah, uh, bye," Logan said.

"No trouble at all, dears. Come back anytime!"

Elena gazed out the window, humming softly to herself as they slipped from the room.

CHAPTER 18

TEO CLIMBED on her bike. "Don't say it."

"Say what?"

"You know. 'I told you so,' or 'sucker.'"

"Look, it's no secret that you were more into this than me, but come on. Elena had us both fooled. She seemed so . . . normal."

"People with mental illnesses or conditions like dementia and Alzheimer's *are* normal," Teo said. "They just have problems. Like we all do."

"You're right," Logan said. "I meant that Elena sounded so rational, even when she talked about

Muma Pădurii. Then suddenly she's joyriding with aliens."

"My great-grandma was like that before she died. Completely rational on every topic except books. She was convinced the novels she read were true and that she was the main character. I felt sad at first, but once our family learned to play along, it was kind of fun. She enjoyed it, so we figured, what's the harm?"

"Makes sense. So . . . we're done with this?"

"With Muma Pădurii? Absolutely."

"And what about the whole kidnapped-babies thing? That too, right?"

Teo looked away and clicked the strap on her bike helmet. "I've got some stuff to do at home. I'll catch you later."

Logan didn't see Teo for three days. Whenever he texted, her response was some version of "I'm busy." He hiked with his mom, then made a triple berry pie with his dad, finally nailing the golden-brown crust. Feeling generous, and bored, he even read a book to Meg.

Logan woke one morning to the chime of an incoming text. He squinted at the sunlight filtering through his blinds and checked his phone. It was Teo.

Can you come over?

He rubbed sleep from his eyes. **Gimme 30 min.**

Logan pulled on his favorite T-shirt, which he'd only worn twice that week, then brushed the gunk from his teeth. He gave some shredded carrots to Flash, his box turtle. After inhaling a microwaved bowl of cinnamon-and-date oatmeal, he biked to Teo's.

He walked into her room and stopped short. Teo stood tapping her chin with a marker and staring at rows of multicolored Post-it notes stuck to a wall.

"Interesting design choice," Logan said.

"Hey. Grab a seat." Teo motioned distractedly to her desk chair, her eyes never leaving the wall.

Logan plopped into the chair, swiveling idly back and forth. "So what's all this?"

She turned to him, her face bright with excitement. "Research."

"It's summer. Why are you doing school stuff?"

Teo rolled her eyes. "Not school stuff. This is important! I was really bummed after talking with Elena, but then it hit me—what if we were on the right track?"

Logan frowned. "But we agreed that Muma Pădurii was a bust."

"Exactly. But what if we had the right idea, just the wrong creature!" She pointed to the grid of sticky notes, each covered with her indecipherable scribbles. "I've been digging into the mythology of other creatures who steal babies. It turns out there's a lot of them. For example, Alpine countries have a creature called Krampus."

"Isn't he some sort of evil Santa Claus dude?" Logan asked.

"Way evil. At Christmas, he'd find kids who misbehaved and beat them with sticks."

"That's disturbing. But as it's the middle of summer, I think we can rule him out."

Teo pointed to another row of notes. "Cronus was a Greek god who ate his own kids."

"And I thought my dad was bad for not raising my allowance. Are we really opening this up to gods now?"

"Of course not. I'm trying to make a point."

"Which is?"

"There are stories about child-stealing creatures from all over the world. While most of them are obviously not true, there must be some basis for them. They're too consistent to be completely made-up. We just have to figure out which creatures could be real, then see if one of them is behind the kidnappings."

Logan crossed his arms. "You're making some pretty big leaps there. Weren't a lot of these kinds of stories made up to keep kids from misbehaving? 'Stay out of the woods, or the fill-in-the-blank monster will get you?'"

"Probably," Teo admitted. "But if there's even a slim chance we could protect more babies, isn't that worth it?" Then she grinned. "Besides, it's fun! What else do you have to do this summer—kill computer aliens?"

"Zombies, actually," Logan said. "But okay, I'll admit this is kind of interesting. Who's next?"

Teo pointed to a row of pink sticky notes. "Fairies are believed to steal babies and replace them with one of their own kind. They're called changelings."

"Our kidnapper hasn't left any strange babies behind. Plus, um, fairies? No."

"Some very serious people have believed in fairies."

"Name one."

"Sir Arthur Conan Doyle."

"The Sherlock Holmes author?"

"Yep. And he was knighted by the king of England and everything."

Logan shook his head. "Just goes to show you, writers are weird."

Teo went through the others on her list, eliminating them one at a time. "And that brings us to the last creature—the Kinderhaken, a type of forest ghoul from German folklore. It's tall and skeletal, with gray skin and fangs. And it sings a creepy melody as it roams the woods at night."

"What makes you think that might be the one?"

"There have been no signs of break-ins at the houses where the babies have been taken, right? Well, the Kinderhaken reaches through windows with a long forked staff and scoops up babies from their cribs. So it wouldn't have to actually enter the house!"

Logan was skeptical, but said, "Okay, I'll bite. How would we find out if this Kinder-thingy is here?"

"It leaves strange footprints near windows where it tries to reach in." She gave Logan a mischievous look.

"Why do I feel like you have a plan I'm not gonna like?"

"Grab your magnifying glass, Watson. We're going to investigate the scene of the crime."

CHAPTER 19

"STOP FIDGETING!" Teo whispered. "Don't you know how to do a stakeout?"

Logan clenched his teeth as he shifted to a more comfortable position behind the bushes near the Dankworths' backyard. The summer sun beat down mercilessly, and bugs crawled up his legs. "Maybe you shouldn't have made us sit on an anthill!"

They peered through the leaves at the house.

"What are we waiting for, anyway?" Logan asked. "There's no one in the yard. Let's just go look."

She gazed at him with an annoyingly superior expression, then spoke like she was quoting a spy manual. "Rushing into a mission without proper surveillance is dangerous. We have to establish the subject's pattern of behavior to learn the best time to approach."

"I think the Dankworths' 'pattern of behavior' is sitting inside their house," Logan grumbled. "Besides, we didn't find anything at the other two houses where babies were taken. What makes you think this one will be any different?"

"It might not be," Teo admitted. "But a good investigator is thorough."

"We could just knock and ask to look in their backyard."

She raised an eyebrow at him. "And when they ask why, then what? Tell them we're looking for monster tracks?" She checked the time on her phone and nodded. "Let's go."

Teo moved off at a crouch with Logan following. They paused at a rear corner of the small brick house. There were three windows in the back wall along with a door leading onto a covered wooden deck. A set of wind chimes dangling from a large overhang played softly in the breeze. Staying low, they padded across the grass until they were beneath the first window. Teo knelt and examined the ground.

"Nothing," she whispered, then pointed up at the window. They stood carefully on either side so they wouldn't be seen through the glass. The wooden shutters and sill looked recently painted. There was no sign the window had been forced open.

They moved cautiously to the next window, but had the same result. The third window was on the opposite side of the glass door leading onto the deck. To reach it, they would have to risk being seen.

Teo crept up to the side of the door and dropped to the ground. Moving like a snake, she crawled across the lawn below the level of the deck, keeping out of sight. Logan rolled his eyes—she looked ridiculous. Reaching the wall on the far side, she stood up and motioned for him to follow.

"I can't believe I'm doing this," he muttered.

A few moments later, he was standing near Teo, rubbing in irritation at a grass stain on his shirt. She crouched down and stared at a flower bed beneath the window. Logan heard a gasp and glanced over. Teo's mouth was open. Wordlessly, she pointed at a gap between two clumps of flowers.

In the dark earth was a strange impression. It appeared old but had a vaguely familiar shape. The roof's deep overhang had protected it from the recent rains. Logan bent down for a closer look.

"Is that a . . . ?" he whispered.

"Footprint," Teo finished.

"But the toes are too long. And there are only four of them."

Teo pointed at strange lines extending from the tip of each toe before looking at Logan with wide eyes. "Claws."

Despite the heat, Logan shivered.

Teo stood and edged closer to the window, then peeked inside. "I see a crib. It's the nursery! And look—there are scratch marks on the windowsill!"

Swallowing a lump in his throat, Logan took an unsteady step backward.

A melodious clanging of metal assaulted his ears as he blundered into the wind chimes.

"Run!" Teo hissed.

They sprinted toward a pair of large trees in the backyard. Just as they ducked behind the thick trunks, the rear door banged open. Logan and Teo pressed themselves against the rough bark. Risking a quick glance behind them, Logan spied Mr. Dankworth on the deck, looking around wildly and gripping a golf club like a weapon.

He stepped off the deck and moved into the yard. Logan pulled his head back and squeezed his eyes shut, praying the man wouldn't come far enough to see them. They heard soft footsteps in the grass, coming steadily closer.

The sounds stopped. Seconds ticked by with agonizing slowness. Teo and Logan held their breaths. *Please go away, please go away,* Logan thought.

Then Mr. Dankworth spoke in a gruff voice. "Who's out here?"

CHAPTER 20

TEO AND Logan locked eyes. She pressed a trembling finger to her lips and shook her head.

A long moment later, Mr. Dankworth muttered, "Annoying birds."

They heard him move toward the house, then the back door slammed shut.

Without a word, Logan and Teo bolted from their hiding places like they'd been shot from a cannon. They tore across the lawn and pounded down the sidewalk, not stopping until they'd reached Teo's house two streets over.

"*Now* do you believe me?" she asked as they entered her room.

Logan collapsed on the beanbag chair, his heart still racing from the run. And from narrowly avoiding Mr. Dankworth wrapping a golf club around his head.

"I . . . I don't know," he said.

"What do you mean? You saw the print and the scratches."

"That was definitely some kind of print. But maybe it was from a big dog or something. And the scratches could have been made by squirrels."

Teo gave him a disbelieving look. "Dogs and squirrels? You think the Dankworths' baby was stolen by cute little forest animals?"

"I didn't say that. But the police must have seen that print too, and it doesn't seem like they thought it was anything unusual."

"Of course not! The police are grown-ups. They aren't going to consider anything supernatural. Only kids are smart enough to think of that."

Logan ran a hand through his hair. "Talking about monsters is fun and everything, but convincing me that one of them is behind this is going to take more than a weird print and some scratches."

Teo paced the floor, chewing her lip. "You're right. We need more evidence. So let's find it."

"Find it where?"

She pointed dramatically to one of the Post-it notes in the Kinderhaken row featuring a scribbled picture of a pine tree. "Where else? We go to where it lives—the woods."

Logan groaned. "Remember what we went through on the *last* monster hunt? I said no more woods."

"But that was before the footprint outside the nursery! You know that was no dog. And this whole town is surrounded by a forest. Whatever left that track probably lives there."

He frowned. "How about we forget the whole thing and go swimming?"

"Babies are being stolen, Logan. I know it's probably nothing, but I really think we should check this out." When he still hesitated, Teo added, "Listen—the Kinderhaken is supposed to be nocturnal, so we can go swimming this afternoon, then search the woods at sundown. Deal?" She gave him a cheeky grin and batted her eyelashes. "Please, Logie Wogie?"

He blew out a breath. "You're more stubborn than Bently, you know that? Fine, I surrender."

They spent the afternoon at the community pool, then ate homemade bistec encebollado and tostones with Teo's parents. At sundown, they headed into the woods that lined her backyard. In the shadows beneath the trees, Teo pulled two flashlights from her backpack and handed one to Logan.

"How long are you planning to be out here?" he asked. "Aren't we gonna head back when it gets too dark?"

"Maybe," she said evasively. "Besides, these are for defense too. Bright light is painful to the Kinderhaken."

Logan clicked on his flashlight, and it was surprisingly powerful. He shined it in Teo's eyes.

"Knock it off!" she growled.

"Oooh, is bright light painful to you? Maybe *you're* the Kinderhaken."

"Your face is the Kinderhaken."

They tromped through the trees into the deepening gloom. Evening sounds rose up around them—the chirping of crickets, the rustling of small animals retreating to their dens, the mournful hoot of an owl. As the darkness thickened, an uncomfortably creepy feeling fluttered in Logan's stomach.

He paused at the bottom of a low rise and swatted irritably at a mosquito on his arm. "Well, no sign of a tall skeletal monster with a baby dangling from its staff. I think we're done here."

"Oh, come on. Let's not quit already."

"But what's the plan exactly? Just wander around and hope we run into this thing? These are big woods. Even if it did exist, the odds of finding it are . . ."

Logan fell silent as a branch snapped somewhere in the darkness. They stared into the trees, listening intently. The sounds of brush being pushed aside drifted from the shadows. Something was moving along the top of the rise. Something big.

Logan's heart thundered as Teo's eyes bulged in the glow of their flashlights. The noise grew closer, until it was just above them. Logan fought the urge to run.

The movement stopped. It grew painfully quiet. The night seemed to hold its breath as Logan strained his ears for the smallest sound.

Then he heard it. On the evening breeze came . . . singing. A soft, wordless melody, eerie and melancholy. Like a blade of ice thrust into his gut, Logan remembered Teo saying the Kinderhaken sings as it stalks its prey.

As one, they thrust their flashlights toward the rise. A huge pair of eyes gleamed in the light.

The monster was real.

And it was hunting them.

CHAPTER 21

THE CREATURE glared down at them, unafraid. Logan reflexively covered his face and was about to scream when an unexpected sound cut through the darkness.

Teo's laughter.

Logan dropped his arm in surprise.

"I think we'll live," she said. "Look."

Standing frozen in the light was a deer. The gentle creature's big ears stood at attention as it simply stared at them. Logan sagged with relief. "I almost peed my pants. Why is it just standing there?"

"That's the way deer respond to bright lights—they freeze. Not sure why."

They lowered their flashlights, and the deer ran off.

"But what about the singing?" Logan asked. "You heard that, right?"

"Yeah. It was creepy."

They both fell silent, listening. The quiet music was just audible, floating softly on the night breeze. "I think it's this way," Teo whispered, pointing into the shadows.

She moved through the trees toward the haunting sound. Logan hesitated as fear crept through him once again. Investigating that voice felt like the last thing he wanted to do. But as Teo got farther away, he realized that being alone in these ominous woods was even worse. He hurried after her.

They quietly made their way through the brush. Dead branches seemed to reach out like claws to snag Logan's shirt, making him jump. The music grew steadily louder, but nothing revealed itself in the probing beams of their flashlights.

As they climbed a small rise, Teo hissed and grabbed his arm. A flickering light appeared in the darkness ahead of them. At a motion from Teo, they both clicked off their flashlights and crept slowly closer, eyes fixed on the strange blue glow. The haunting melody swelled to a crescendo, then suddenly stopped.

The sound of applause burst through the night.

Logan and Teo looked at each other in total confusion. He pushed forward, staring hard at the flickering light. As his eyes adjusted from turning off their flashlights, the dim outline of a house appeared through the trees. Through an open sliding door, the blue glow resolved itself into a television screen showing people clapping for a performer on a stage.

In the dark, they had unknowingly circled back toward the row of houses. They were staring at one of Teo's neighbors. Logan's relief was mingled with frustration, and he turned to Teo with an exasperated sigh. "The only monsters out here are these stupid vampire mosquitoes! I'm out."

He stomped away in the direction of Teo's house. With a reluctant glance back into the brooding woods, Teo followed him.

From high in a nearby tree, a pair of glowing green eyes watched them go.

CHAPTER 22

FOR LOGAN, the next few days were wonderfully normal, with hours spent playing *Zombie Hunter* and reading Castle Dread graphic novels. He didn't even mind mowing the lawn and helping his dad cook dinner.

He'd just finished a breakfast of frozen waffles topped with strawberry jam and whipped cream when he got a text from Teo.

Wanna hang out?

Logan texted back: **K. See you in 15.**

Teo was hunched over her computer when he walked into her room. "Hey," she said without turning around.

Logan glanced over her shoulder at a strange image on her screen. It looked like a demented chimpanzee with a weird beak and glowing green eyes.

"What the heck is that?"

"It's called a snatcher," Teo said excitedly. "They're listed in this article on mythological creatures."

"And you're reading about them why?"

"They're called snatchers because they steal babies!"

Logan gave Teo a hard look. "We've struck out twice. *Three* times if you count the hospital. I thought we were done with the whole baby thing?"

"*You* were. I couldn't stop thinking about it. I've been doing more research, and last night I found this!"

Logan ran a hand through his thick blond hair.

"You are seriously exhausting me here. What about the Kinderhaken?"

"I read yesterday that its hands and feet are like a human's—no claws. The print we found had claw marks, so that rules out the Kinderhaken."

Logan glanced back at the creature on the screen. "So you think the Dankworths' baby was taken by a creepy imaginary monkey?"

"Don't judge me for having an open mind."

"Open? I think your brain just fell out."

"Whatever. The woman who wrote this article also wrote a book on monster lore, and there's a whole chapter on snatchers." She closed her laptop. "Up for a trip to Banshee?"

Banshee Books was one of Logan and Teo's favorite hangouts. There were lots of comfy chairs and colorful, book-themed murals on the walls. The owner,

Regina, always sported a bandana over her long locs and wore jewelry she made from things other people had thrown away. To Logan, she was one of the rare grown-ups who looked kids in the eye and actually listened when they talked. Her Siamese cat, Nefertiti, reigned over the bookstore like the Egyptian ruler she was named for.

"Here it is!" Teo said, pulling a book from a shelf. *"Monster Lore: A Complete Guide to Things That Go Bump in the Night* by Jesenia Ayad. Got any cash?"

"Yeah, from babysitting Meg," Logan said. "But you're buying the ice cream."

They bought the book, then headed across the street to Moo Magic. Logan went for his usual, a Moo Mash-Up with M&M'S and cookie dough, while Teo got mocha gelato.

Their stomachs now content, they biked back to Logan's house and sat shoulder to shoulder on the oversized chair in his room. Flash the turtle dozed in her miniature pool at the end of her tank. Teo flipped to the chapter on snatchers, and the same drawing they'd seen online filled the opening page.

"Aha!" Teo exclaimed a few moments later, stabbing her finger on the text. "'Snatchers are notorious for sneaking into homes at night and stealing babies from their cribs while the unsuspecting parents are asleep,'" she read, then turned to Logan. "In my research over the last few days, I found out that *all three* babies were taken from their cribs at night, not just the Dankworths'. So this fits the pattern!"

"Teo, we've been through this," he said. "This is a *mythology* book. It's just like Muma Pădurii and the Kinderhaken—snatchers don't exist."

"Almost everyone said that big, hairy, manlike creatures in African jungles didn't exist either. And then scientists officially recognized mountain gorillas in the 1900s."

"Really? Okay, I didn't know about the gorilla thing. But that doesn't mean snatchers are real."

"True, but look at this—it says they migrate, appear unexpectedly, and live in remote caves in heavily wooded areas. This whole town is surrounded by a forest. And I bet there are caves in Falcon Ridge. You've gotta admit, it's possible."

"Sure, in the same way Bigfoot is possible. Which would be really cool, by the way. But I'm not sold."

"Neither am I," Teo said. "But I think it's worth checking out."

Logan wanted to object, but decided to bite his lip and keep reading. "Looks like we don't have to worry about them stealing our Doritos. It says they can't even step across a line of salt."

"Who can't step across salt?" said a voice from the doorway.

Logan glanced over at Meg. "Go away."

Ignoring him, Meg wandered in and looked over

their shoulders. She pointed to the snatcher picture. "I like him. He's cute."

"It isn't cute," Teo said. "Those things are evil."

"Evil?" said Meg. "Why?"

"Never mind," Logan said. "We don't want to scare you."

"Me? I'm not scared. You're the one who's afraid of everything."

He pointed to the door. "Out. We've got serious stuff to talk about."

"Fine! I'll go play with Ollie!" She stomped from the room.

Logan turned back to the book with a sigh. "I wish the snatcher would take *her*."

CHAPTER 23

THE NEXT day, Logan gazed wearily at the endless trees and swiped at a dive-bombing mosquito. It was another sweltering day, and he was mad at himself for letting Teo talk him into searching the woods again. The ten dollars in arcade tokens she'd bribed him with didn't feel worth it anymore. "Why are we doing this?"

"Missing. *Babies*," Teo said. "How many times do I have to say it before you get how serious this is?"

"Yeah, I know that. But I don't see how aimlessly

wandering the woods day after day is gonna help. Besides, I'm allergic to poison ivy." He stepped farther away from a suspicious-looking plant.

"Everyone's allergic to poison ivy, genius."

"Actually, no. About fifteen percent of people are immune."

"And you know this why?"

"Because I'm *way* allergic. I once had poison ivy so bad that my face was covered with oozing sores. I woke up one morning with my cheek stuck to the pillow."

Teo scrunched up her nose. "Eww."

"Yep. So if you don't want to be best friends with Quasimodo, let's wrap this up."

She put her hands on her hips. "Urgh! There are supposed to be caves around here. I read in a hiking blog that they're in a really gnarly section of woods."

"Did you just say 'gnarly'? As in 'Yo, dude, let's snarf fish tacos and catch some waves'?"

Teo was not amused. "Ten more minutes. If we don't find anything, we can leave."

Logan started a timer on his phone, then trudged along as she walked off with a determined stride. He thought that was a good word for Teo—*determined.* Which is a nice way of saying "stubborn." She was more stubborn than Bently—at least the bulldog let go of his shoe when he rubbed her belly.

Not soon enough for Logan, his phone chimed. "That's ten minutes. We haven't found anything, so we're outta here."

"Look again," Teo said.

Ahead of them stood a dark patch of trees, so thick and choked with brambles that the late-afternoon sun barely penetrated. An ominous feeling seemed to radiate from its depths.

Logan swallowed uncomfortably. "That looks . . ."

"Gnarly?" Teo asked.

Point to Teo, Logan thought as she began pushing

her way into the shadows. "Whoa, wait, really?" he asked. "I mean, do we have to?"

"This is the place we've been looking for! Where the caves are supposed to be. If you were a snatcher, wouldn't you live in a place like this?"

Logan tried to imagine himself as a demented, baby-stealing monkey. Fortunately, he failed. As Teo surged ahead with renewed energy, he muttered under his breath and followed.

It wasn't the same once they entered the dark section of woods—it was worse. The gloom pressed in on them like a living thing. The air was heavy and oppressive, without a hint of breeze. Vines and creepers hung from eerie-looking trees with twisted roots and long branches that reached out like skeleton arms. It was unnervingly quiet. Animals seemed to avoid this part of the forest.

Logan stopped and glanced back the way they'd come. He couldn't see their path. Everything looked the same. The sense of unease that had been growing in him swelled to low-level panic. Demonic monkeys now seemed completely plausible. Along with Bigfoot, aliens, and every creature in every horror movie ever. *Time to go.*

"I need to get out of here," Logan said. "Teo?"

She was gone.

For a moment, he stood still, not daring to breathe.

Then something grabbed Logan's shoulder, and he let out a bloodcurdling scream.

CHAPTER 24

LOGAN WHIRLED to face the monster attacking him. If he was about to die, he wanted to go down fighting.

The "monster" was three and a half feet tall with blond pigtails. And she was laughing.

"I got you so good!" Meg said. "You should have seen your face!"

"Nice scream," Teo said, emerging from a nearby clump of trees. "Bently probably heard you all the way back home."

"M-Meg!" Logan sputtered, his face hot with embarrassment. "What are you doing here? You shouldn't have followed us!"

"I can do what I want!" she said, glaring up at him.

"No, you can't," he said, still trying to recover his composure. "You're a little kid. You could get lost out here."

"I am not little! And I won't get lost. I've been out here plenty of times."

"Why are you here, Meg?" Teo asked.

"Mom says to come home for dinner," she said, looking at Logan like *she* was the older sibling. "Bye, Teo." Meg stuck out her tongue at Logan and marched through the woods in the direction of their neighborhood.

He watched her go with a scowl. Teo laughed. "That kid sure has guts," she said. "And that *was* pretty funny."

"You don't have to live with her. And no, it wasn't."

"I guess we should go," she said, sounding disappointed. "I really wish we could look around some more."

"That makes one of us," Logan said darkly. He stalked after Meg, and Teo followed.

Behind a nearby tree, a dark shape stood motionless as it listened to their footsteps die away. Reaching out, it used the thick bark to sharpen its claws.

CHAPTER 25

LATE THAT night, the creature slid through the shadows beneath a maze of trees.

As it crossed a clearing, a gust of wind ruffled its coat of jet-black hair. Beneath the scents of honeysuckle and pine, it detected the fading stench of the humans.

The creature shifted its burden as it maneuvered easily over a fallen tree. A weak cry came from the bundle of cloth it carried.

The cry of a baby.

CHAPTER 26

THE NEXT morning, Logan stumbled down the hall with a yawn. He was about to enter the kitchen when he heard his parents talking softly and paused to listen.

"I can't believe it happened again," Logan's mom said.

"I'm getting scared," said Logan's dad.

Logan swallowed hard. He could guess what they were talking about. Feeling a little guilty for eavesdropping, he walked into the kitchen. His mom immediately set her phone facedown on the table as his dad looked up quickly, a fake smile plastered on his face.

"Morning," he said. "Ready for breakfast?"

Logan hesitated. "Was another baby taken?"

The smile melted from his father's face as his parents glanced at each other. His mom turned to Logan. "Yes, I'm afraid so. How much do you know about this?"

Logan told them about the conversation with Mrs. Dankworth and the flyer they'd seen in the thrift store window. He decided not to mention anything else. He was pretty sure they wouldn't want him looking into the abductions, and knew they'd be even more skeptical of the evil-monkey-creature theory than he was.

"That was really kind of you to return the stroller," his mom said.

"And to listen to her story," his dad said. "That poor

woman. I can't imagine what she's going through. Are you okay?"

Logan shrugged. "Yeah, I guess. I mean, I feel really bad for those parents."

His dad nodded. "If you ever want to talk about it, we're here. I'll be honest, it's rattled us."

His mom wore a worried frown. "I'm sure the police will catch whoever's behind this soon, but until then, stay close to home, okay?"

"And don't tell Meg," his dad said. "We don't want to frighten her." He gave his wife an anxious look, then turned back to Logan. "We're not sure if they're only after babies."

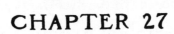

CHAPTER 27

"BUT DON'T you see?" Teo asked later that morning. "This means we *have* to go back."

They were sitting in Teo's backyard playing with Bently. Logan had just finished telling her about the conversation with his parents.

"But what about staying close to home?" he asked. "I don't like sneaking around behind my parents' backs."

"I get that. But it's *still happening.* Now *four* babies are missing! Maybe it's not a snatcher behind it, but I guarantee we're the only ones even considering that. The police can do their thing, and we'll do ours. It may not help, but we have to try."

Logan rubbed his temples with the heels of his hands and sighed. "Okay. But maybe we should tell our parents."

"Think about it," Teo said, mindlessly tossing the ball for Bently to chase. "If we say anything about a monster, they'll blow it off as ridiculous *and* double down on keeping us out of the woods. We can't risk it."

Logan moodily yanked up bits of grass. "Fine. We'll go search the creepy place again. But this time we bring snacks. *And* Bently."

The bulldog ran up wearing her usual big grin and dropped the slobbery ball in his lap. Teo attached a leash to Bently's collar, then filled a backpack with snacks and water bottles. After telling Teo's mom they were taking Bently for a walk, they headed into the woods behind her house.

Bently lumbered from tree to tree, joyfully sniffing and squatting to mark her territory. Logan didn't share her enthusiasm. He knew they were doing the right thing but couldn't shake the feeling that something ominous hovered over them like a storm cloud. A storm cloud made of broken glass and killer bees.

Now that they knew where to go, they all too quickly reached the eerie section of the woods. Bently whined uncertainly.

"See?" Logan said. "Even she doesn't like this place."

"Come on, girl," Teo said, urging the bulldog forward.

They wound their way through the dim trees, farther than they'd gone before. The thick underbrush made for slow going, especially with stopping to untangle Bently's leash. After pushing through a particularly difficult patch, they emerged into a small clearing near the base of Falcon Ridge, the mountain behind their neighborhood.

"How about a break?" Logan said. He was panting almost as much as Bently, and his arms were covered with scratches. They sat on a log and opened the backpack. After giving Bently some water, Teo let the bulldog wander the dismal clearing with her leash dragging behind her.

"Killer spot," Logan said through a mouthful of M&M'S. "I think I'll build a tree fort here."

Teo looked around glumly and sighed. "Maybe you were right. There doesn't seem to be anything in this mess."

"At least we tried," he said.

She nodded, but still looked disappointed.

Bently growled, and Logan glanced up. The bulldog was pressed halfway into a bush on the far side of the clearing.

"What is it, girl?" Teo asked as they walked over. She pushed aside the top of the bush, and they peered into the gloom.

A flash of movement caught Logan's eye, something dark and fast. It shot from behind a tree and disappeared toward the mountain.

Even from a glimpse, he knew it was nothing he'd ever seen before.

"Did you see that?" he exclaimed.

"Yeah," Teo said, a slight tremor in her voice. Logan guessed she was excited rather than afraid. Unlike him. "Come on!" She grabbed Bently's leash and hurried in the direction the thing had gone. Forcing his trembling legs to move, Logan ran after her.

Nose to the ground, Bently tugged Teo forward, finally stopping at the base of the ridge. The dog gave another low growl and peered fixedly ahead.

Near the ground was a low, dark opening.

"It's a cave!" Teo said.

They bent down and peered inside. Teo pulled out her phone and pointed the flashlight at the entrance.

The dim light didn't penetrate far, but the dirt on the cave floor looked recently disturbed.

"Should we go in?" Teo asked. She sounded uncertain, which didn't help Logan's mood.

"Without real flashlights?"

At that moment, Bently, who had pushed forward into the opening, whimpered and backed away. She turned and pulled on her leash, desperate to get away from the cave.

Logan looked at Teo for a heartbeat. Then they scrambled up and raced back through the clearing toward home.

CHAPTER 28

"SO, REALLY, what do you think it was?" Teo asked an hour later as they sat in their favorite corner booth at Moo Magic.

Logan clenched his jaws. "For the fourth time, *I don't know*. It happened too fast."

"Neither of us recognized it, so it wasn't a dog. Too small for a bear. And bobcats don't have black hair."

Logan pushed moodily at his sundae. Even a Moo Mash-Up with double whipped cream wasn't making him feel any better.

"So it could have been, you know, a *snatcher*," Teo

continued, whispering the last word conspiratorially.
"Don't you think?"

He glared at her. "If you make me say 'I don't know' one more time, I'm dumping this ice cream on your head."

She crossed her arms and blew out an exasperated breath. "So mature. And really helpful. We have to talk about this so we can decide what to do when we go out there again."

"Out there again?" he growled. "Maybe I don't *wanna* go out there again."

"But, Logan, we have to! The babies—"

"Stop telling me what I have to do!" He slammed his spoon loudly on the table. "I don't care about the babies, okay? I'm just a kid! I want my summer back, and I'm tired—" The final, ugly truth caught in his throat. He didn't want say it, but knew he needed to. Logan focused on a scratch in the table, unable to meet Teo's eyes. "I'm tired of being afraid."

Teo stared at him in disbelief. "Hey, I'm scared

too, but that doesn't get us off the hook. And you *want your summer back*? Seriously? I can't believe you're that selfish."

Logan's face flushed as a wave of heat surged through his body. "*I'm* selfish? Oh, that's hilarious coming from you. Who is it that always gets their way, huh? If you haven't noticed, it's *you*! I go along with whatever your latest obsession is because if I don't, I'll never hear the end of it! But not this time." Logan stood up, so angry he was trembling. He realized people were staring, but he didn't care. "You wanna hunt monsters? Fine. But you can do it without me!"

Stomping to the exit, he flung open the door and stormed out.

CHAPTER 29

"YAY! I won again!" Meg cried as she slid her piece across the board, then clapped happily.

Logan lay back on the living room rug and watched the ceiling fan spin lazily. It had been three days since his blowup with Teo, and, desperate for something to do, he'd resorted to hanging out with Meg.

"Teo should come play with us," she said. "You're not very good at games."

"Well, you don't have to worry about that any-more." He got to his feet and headed down the hall. "I'm done."

"Wait! Don't quit. I take it back!"

Logan closed his bedroom door and flopped onto his bed. He tried reading a graphic novel but couldn't concentrate. Wandering over to the glass tank on his dresser, he picked up his turtle. "You like me, don't you, Flash?"

She pooped on his hand.

"Everything stinks!" Logan grumbled, grabbing a dirty sock from the floor and wiping his palm. He rested his elbows on the windowsill and stared at the woods that lined his backyard. He used to love that view, but now the trees seemed menacing. "Thanks a lot, summer," he mumbled. Logan was a champion at feeling sorry for himself.

Meg wandered into the backyard pushing one of her dolls in a toy stroller. *Lucky kid,* Logan thought. *She doesn't have a care in the world.*

Then a different stroller popped into his mind. An empty one, abandoned alongside the road. The image of Mrs. Dankworth came back to him with startling clarity. Her tearstained face. Her trembling voice. Her hopeless words. What must it be like to have your child snatched away? Logan couldn't imagine. Or maybe he didn't want to.

Yet here he stood, feeling like *he* was the victim. Maybe Teo was right. Maybe he was selfish. He definitely felt like a coward, at least compared with her. Only a scared kid? True. But did that free him from helping those grieving families? Especially if he might be one of the only ones who could?

Logan slowly blew out a deep breath, then picked up his phone.

An hour later, Teo and Logan sat on the grassy bank of the Crane River, which gently flowed behind the downtown shops. Bently snoozed in a nearby patch of sun.

Logan tossed a rock into the water and watched the current smooth out the ripples. "So what I'm trying to say is, you were right. I'm a coward, and I'm being selfish about the whole baby thing. Sorry I blew up at you and stormed off like that."

"Thanks," Teo said softly. "But you're not the only one who needs to apologize. You were right, too. When there's something I wanna do, I keep pushing until I force you to go along with it. That's not cool." She picked a dandelion and twirled it between her fingers. "And you're not a coward. Scared, maybe. But sometimes it's smart to be scared."

"Then I must be a genius."

"Absolutely. A regular Albert Einstein."

They glanced at each other, and both cracked a smile.

"Are we good?" she asked.

"We're good." Logan paused a moment, then took a deep breath. "So. Are you ready to go back in the woods?"

CHAPTER 30

"BENTLY, COME on!" Teo said.

The bulldog strained at her leash, trying desperately to reach a squirrel who chittered mockingly at her from a low branch.

The late-afternoon sun slanted through the trees, giving the woods an otherworldly feel. To show Teo he was serious about his change of heart, Logan had suggested coming straight from the riverbank to do a quick search before dark. But as they entered the menacing section of the woods, his enthusiasm waned. *Too late to back out now.*

They pushed through a thorny thicket sporting red berries flecked with black spots. Logan imagined they tempted you with their color only to kill you with their poison. Nursing fresh scratches, they pressed further into the gloom. The dense canopy shut out the light, and the thick brush blocked the breeze. The silence was heavy. Even the birds had abandoned this place.

Bently's playful attitude had dropped away. She whined, moving reluctantly as Teo half dragged her forward. Logan kept glancing over his shoulder as the hairs on the back of his neck prickled. It felt like they were being watched.

Something sharp and strong clawed his arm. Logan lurched forward with a choked cry and whirled to see . . .

Nothing.

"It's okay," Teo said, pointing to a quivering dead tree limb. "You caught yourself on a branch."

The fact that she wasn't making fun of him showed

she was scared too. But almost having a heart attack over a tree limb *was* kind of funny. Logan grinned sheepishly. Teo's mouth tugged up into a smile. A moment later, they both cracked up, letting laughter wash away the tension.

When they'd calmed down, Teo said, "Here, take Bently. My shoe's untied."

She handed Logan the leash and bent to tie her shoe. The bulldog's whimpering increased, then Bently started pulling Logan toward home.

A moment later, Teo screamed.

Logan spun around. She lay flat on her stomach, arms outstretched, a look of horror on her face. Something hidden in the brush was dragging Teo by her feet. As Logan stood frozen in shock, she disappeared into the shadowy undergrowth.

"Logan!" she screamed.

Her cry snapped him into action. Dropping Bently's leash, he hurtled through the brush, following the sounds of struggle. Bently howled and bolted for home.

Logan burst into a familiar clearing and slid to a stop. On the far side lay Teo, stretched full out, her hands locked around the trunk of a small tree. Tugging wildly at her feet was a horrifying creature. It looked like a demonic chimpanzee, with thick black hair and a beaklike muzzle. Triangular ears were pressed flat against its skull, and its long, clawed fingers were clamped on Teo's ankle.

Teo sobbed for help, her eyes like saucers. Glancing around frantically, Logan grabbed a stick and sprinted toward the creature with a terrified yell. Raising the improvised weapon over his head, he swung it as hard as he could. The creature leaped aside at the last instant. The stick hit the ground and snapped in half.

For a long moment, the creature glared at Logan with glowing emerald eyes.

Then, with a hiss of rage, it scurried into the cave and disappeared.

CHAPTER 31

"I'VE NEVER run so fast in my entire life," Logan said.

In the comforting safety of his room, he raised a water bottle to his lips, his trembling hand sending a trickle down his chin. Bently, worn out from their adventure, snored noisily in the corner.

"Still wondering if snatchers are real?" Teo asked, her face ashen.

Logan shook his head. "I wish I was. That thing looked pretty close to the picture in the book. But *way* scarier in real life."

"You're telling me. Thanks, by the way. You were really brave back there."

"Was I? Honestly, I didn't even think. I was too terrified."

"That's what bravery is, right? Being scared but doing the right thing anyway."

Logan shrugged, then tore open a pack of cherry Pop-Tarts. He took a bite and let the sugary sprinkles dissolve on his tongue.

Teo looked thoughtful. "Now that we know there really is a snatcher out there, I think we should tell our parents."

"That's ironic—I was just thinking the opposite. I mean, what are we going to say? That you were attacked by a monster? They'll never believe us. Besides, I'll get in trouble for being that far from home."

"Yeah, but what happens if we don't tell? That thing could steal another kid."

Logan remembered the heartbreak in Mrs. Dankworth's voice. "You're right. We've got to try." He checked his phone. "My mom will be home from work soon. We'll do it then."

An hour later, they heard the garage door open, followed by the murmur of conversation.

"You got this," Teo said. "I'll back you up."

Logan's stomach clenched as they walked into the kitchen. His dad was setting some pans on the stove. "Hey, you two. Teo, can you stay for dinner?"

"Thanks. I'll check with my parents, but I'm sure it's fine."

Logan's mom put down the stack of mail she'd been sorting. "What's up? You both look pretty serious."

Logan glanced at Teo, who nodded encouragingly. "Well . . . I, um . . . I mean, we . . . have something to tell you." Haltingly, with Teo filling in the gaps, Logan told his parents about their research, exploring the woods, and finally, the snatcher attack on Teo.

To their credit, his parents didn't interrupt. They did exchange a few troubled glances.

Logan finished weakly with "So we wanted you to know . . . and stuff."

His dad was the first to speak. "That's quite a story. I'm not sure where to begin."

"First off, are you both okay?" his mom asked. "You're pretty scratched up."

"Yeah, we're fine," Logan said.

She nodded. "Okay, next, I'm disappointed in you, Logan. I thought we were pretty clear about you staying close to home."

Oof, he thought. *The disappointed line. I'd rather have them yell at me.* "Yeah, I know. And I'm really sorry, but—"

"But what?" his dad asked. "You both put yourselves in danger. These abductions are very serious."

"But that's why we wanted to help!" Logan said. "*Because* they're serious. And we figured out something no one else did."

"That a mythological creature you read about on-line is stealing those babies?" his mom asked, her eyebrow arched.

"The thing that grabbed me was no myth," Teo said quietly.

Logan's parents looked at each other for a long moment. He could tell they were having one of their silent conversations. *Annoying.* Finally, his mom turned to them. "I love that you both have active imaginations . . ."

"And that you wanted to help," his dad said.

"But that's what it was—your imaginations," his mom said. "I'm sure you did see something, like a dog or even a small black bear—"

"It wasn't a *dog*!" Logan said, his voice rising.

"And in the dark woods," his mom continued, ignoring his outburst, "your imaginations turned it into this creature you were looking for."

"It's not uncommon," his dad said. "Our brains can easily trick our sense of sight."

"I know what I saw," Logan said, his jaw tight.

His mom glanced at her husband. "We believe that you believe that. But that doesn't make it true."

Logan opened his mouth to fire back, but Teo nudged him and shook her head. "Let it go," she whispered. He blew out a frustrated breath and bit his cheek.

"While we applaud your good intentions," his dad said, "we don't want you anywhere near the woods until this is over. Got it?"

Both parents looked at Logan, waiting for an answer. He nodded stiffly.

"Good," his mom said. "Now we have news for you. Grandma Jean is sick again, and it's pretty bad this time. She can't be alone, so Dad and I are driving up to stay with her for a few days. You and Meg are going to Aunt Roslyn's."

"Sorry about Grandma. Can I stay with Teo?"

"No," his mom said. "We need you to help watch Meg. Roslyn has her hands full with Gabby."

Logan got the feeling that was only part of the reason. They weren't about to give him something he wanted right after he'd disobeyed them. Still, he wasn't giving up without a fight.

"Meg's old enough. She'll be—"

Surprisingly, Teo cut him off. "Maybe it's *good* for you to be there," she said carefully. "I mean, Meg's still a little kid, and your cousin's only a baby . . ." She raised her eyebrows meaningfully.

Logan got the message, and his shoulders slumped.

Time for guard duty.

CHAPTER 32

LATER THAT evening, moonlight filled Meg's bedroom with a gentle glow.

As she slept, the silence was broken by a soft scrape as the window facing the woods eased gently aside. Claws appeared in the opening. In one fluid motion, the snatcher pulled itself noiselessly onto the window ledge.

The creature paused, watching the sleeping girl. A soft murmur, almost a purr, came from its beaklike muzzle. It lowered itself to the carpet and padded stealthily over to the bed. In the pale light, the snatcher's dark hair appeared midnight blue as it stretched its hands toward Meg.

At the sound of footsteps, the snatcher hesitated, looking up sharply. Seconds later, it darted out the open window as the bedroom door creaked open. Meg's father entered and gazed down at his daughter. He smoothed her blanket and placed a soft kiss on her forehead.

As he turned to go, he noticed the curtains swaying in the breeze. He shut and locked the window, then slipped out, quietly closing the door behind him.

In the backyard, the snatcher watched him from its perch in a towering maple. It studied the dark window for a long moment. Then the creature leaped. Catching a nearby limb, it swung from tree to tree, peering into neighboring houses with piercing green eyes.

CHAPTER 33

THE NEXT day, Meg and her friends Jack and Lily were loudly playing Gnomes at Night in Aunt Roslyn's living room.

"You should ask your friend Ollie to come," Lily said to Meg. "Then we could play teams!"

Logan came in from the hallway. "Keep it down, will you? You'll wake up Gabby."

"We don't have to listen to you," Meg said. She stuck out her tongue, then went back to the game.

Kids these days, Logan thought. *No respect.*

As predicted, Gabby began crying. Aunt Roslyn called from the kitchen, "Logan, can you grab her? I'm making lunch."

With a sigh, he headed to the nursery. Gabby lay in her crib, waving her little fists in the air, and her pudgy cheeks were red. Removing her blue pony-print blanket, he picked her up and cradled her like a football, supporting her head the way he'd been taught. She stopped crying and gazed at Logan like he was the most fascinating thing in the world. As far as baby cousins went, Gabby was pretty cool.

"I want to hold her!" Meg said from the doorway.

"No, you're too little."

"I am not! I'm good with babies. *Please?*"

Aunt Roslyn appeared behind her. "Thanks, Logan. I can take her now. Meg, I brought lunch out for you and your friends."

Meg clapped happily and ran back to the living room. Logan handed Gabby off to Aunt Roslyn, then went to the kitchen, where his food waited on the table. As he added salt to the T in his BLT sandwich, he had an idea. Checking to make sure Aunt Roslyn was in the living room, he entered the pantry and scanned the shelves. Spotting a large container of salt, he grabbed it and slipped down the hall.

In the nursery, Logan carefully poured a thick line of salt along the windowsill. He did the same thing in the room he shared with Meg. If the book was right about a snatcher not being able to cross salt, maybe this was all the protection Gabby needed. But he couldn't afford to take chances.

Logan returned the salt container without being spotted, then ate three sandwiches and snuck extra cookies for later. He had a long night ahead.

That evening, after everyone was asleep, Logan crept down the hall and eased open the door to Gabby's nursery. As annoying as he found Meg, he didn't like leaving her alone, but Gabby was more vulnerable. And if the snatcher did target Meg, hopefully the salt would prevent it from entering.

He moved quietly to a rocking chair in the corner and settled in. At first, it was a little exciting, staring at the window, guarding his baby cousin from a strange and horrible creature that stalked the neighborhood.

But pretty soon, it was just boring. Logan yawned and checked the time—12:17 a.m. He ate some cookies and played a silent game on his phone. His head kept drooping, and his eyelids felt like they were coated with concrete. Eventually, he nodded off.

Logan heard a noise like claws on glass. Something was trying to get in. He looked up. There! He could see it! The snatcher's face was outside the window, its glowing green eyes piercing him with an evil glare. The window slid aside—

Logan's head jerked up, and he looked frantically toward the window.

The glass pane was empty.

His heart still galloping, he slumped back in the rocking chair and sighed with relief. It was only a nightmare. He took a deep breath, trying to calm himself.

Then Logan heard a scraping sound outside the window. He peered intently but couldn't see anything. When it came again, he gave his leg a sharp pinch. *Yep, definitely awake this time.* Crouching low, he scuttled across the carpet until he was directly beneath the window.

The sound came again.

Trembling with dread, Logan lifted his head and peeked out.

He barely stifled a scream.

CHAPTER 34

LOGAN COVERED his mouth and stumbled backward onto his butt.

His eyes locked on a tree branch, scraping lightly against the window as it swayed in the breeze. He lay back on the carpet, breathing heavily.

At least Teo didn't see that, he thought.

Fortunately, he'd managed to scare himself quietly, so Gabby was still sleeping peacefully. He stood and put a hand to his chest. His heart thumped, and his forehead was slick with sweat. The nursery air felt warm and stagnant.

Logan slipped down the hallway and through the kitchen. Easing the back door open, he stepped onto the deck. The cool night breeze felt wonderful, and he closed his eyes, soaking it in.

Then he remembered where he was, and his eyes flew open. The sky was filled with clusters of stars, and the full moon cast harsh shadows across the lawn. Was the snatcher affected by the lunar cycle like a werewolf? Was it out there somewhere gazing up at the same moon?

Logan glanced around uneasily, uncomfortable being outside alone. *It was only a tree branch,* he reminded himself. He took a deep breath, but it didn't help. Shifting nervously, he imagined a clawed hand reaching from beneath the deck to grab his ankle. He hurried inside and locked the door behind him, then backed away, gazing through the window at the empty deck. "Get a grip," he whispered.

Returning to the rocking chair in the nursery, he set a vibration alarm on his phone in case he fell asleep again. But as amped up as he felt now, that didn't seem likely.

Logan gazed at Gabby nestled in her crib. What did she think about when she was awake? *Did* babies think? One thing was for sure—she wasn't worried about a monster. No evil creature haunted her dreams. He rubbed his temples wearily. *I never thought I'd be jealous of a baby.*

After what seemed like only a moment, Logan felt a buzzing in his lap and looked down in confusion. Why was his phone buzzing already? He checked the time, and four hours had passed. He'd fallen asleep after all. His eyes darted to Gabby, and he sighed with relief.

Out the window, the sky above the woods was tinged with pink. They'd made it through the night.

Logan quietly returned to the guest bedroom, where Meg was lightly snoring. He flopped onto his bed and fell instantly asleep.

Logan felt a hand shaking his shoulder.

"Come on," Meg said. "You've been sleeping forever."

"Mwph," he grumbled, and turned his back to her. "Go away."

"But I'm *bored*. Let's do something."

"Go play with Lily and Jack."

"They can't come over, and neither can Ollie." She switched to a singsong voice. "Aunt Roslyn made pancakes."

He lifted his head slightly. "With chocolate chips?"

"And powdered sugar," Meg said. "Better come quick if you want any, 'cause I'm *really* hungry." She giggled and ran from the room.

Logan stumbled out of bed and, after a trip to the bathroom, yawned his way to the kitchen.

"Glad you could join us, Rip Van Winkle," Aunt Roslyn said.

"Huh?" Logan asked, his face scrunched in confusion.

"Ugh, you make me feel old. Never mind. Help yourself."

Pulling pancakes onto his plate, Logan smothered them with butter and syrup, then took a bite of the warm, fluffy goodness. "Tanks, Aunt Woslyn," he said around a huge mouthful. "These oww awesome."

"You're welcome. And you can do something for me. I need a little quiet so I can put Gabby down for her morning nap. Why don't you take Meg to the park?"

Logan barely succeeded in hiding his groan. He just wanted to lie in bed and read Raptor Man graphic novels. But knowing he was stuck, he nodded.

"Yay!" Meg said. "Park! Park! Park!"

Logan rolled his eyes. It was going to be a long morning.

Half an hour later, he and Meg were on a swing set. Logan sat motionless with his cheek resting against the chain, wishing it were a pillow.

"Push me!" Meg said.

"No."

"You're boring."

"Nope. Just tired."

"Why?"

"Never mind, you wouldn't understand."

"I would too! I'm not a little kid."

"You are a little kid."

Logan pulled out his phone and texted Teo: **Meet at the park?**

She replied a few seconds later: **See you in 15.**

With a sigh, he hauled himself to his feet and pushed Meg on the swings. Then he chased her while she ran screaming in delight. Finally, they played on the teeter-totter. He tried to be a good big brother. Sometimes.

Teo showed up, and she and Logan climbed to the top of the monkey bars. When Meg tried to follow, he said, "Sorry, Meg. I need to talk to Teo alone, okay?"

She looked disappointed, but surprisingly, she nodded and went to the slide. *Huh,* Logan thought. *Maybe I should be nice to her more often.*

Teo gave him an appraising glance. "You look terrible."

"Thank you," he said through a yawn.

"Anything to report?"

He told her everything that had happened last night, leaving out that a tree branch had made him fall on his butt.

She looked thoughtful. "We know a snatcher is behind this, right?"

"Yeah," said Logan. "But no one believes us."

"Then we'll have to get proof."

"How do we do that?"

"We'll go back to the cave and look for footprints, a clump of hair snagged in a bush, whatever. If we're lucky, maybe we can get a photo."

"Being close enough to that thing to get a photo doesn't sound lucky to me," Logan said, trying to tame his bedhead with his hands. "Besides, you heard my parents. They'll ground me for life if I go out there again."

"Not if we help stop the kidnappings."

"That's a big if." Logan chewed his lip. Imagining his parents finding out he'd returned to the woods made his stomach clench. And the thought of being face-to-face with the snatcher filled him with cold dread.

Then Logan remembered Gabby sleeping peacefully in her crib. Was that how the other babies looked before they were taken? What would he be feeling right now if he'd woken up and found her missing? He'd be out of his mind. Frantic. Desperate. Crushed. If there was anything he could do to save a family from that horror, he had to try.

"So when do we go?" he asked.

"How about now?"

Logan shook his head. "I have to babysit Meg until my parents get back tomorrow. And Aunt Roslyn would get suspicious if I disappeared for a few hours."

"Okay, tomorrow. It's only one more night. We should be fine until then."

Logan tried to ignore the gnawing feeling that she was terribly wrong.

CHAPTER 35

"WHUH? WHAT?" Logan sat up sharply in the rocking chair and looked in the crib. Gabby was fast asleep.

Just like *he'd* been a minute ago.

He checked his phone—2:28 a.m. Despite his best efforts, he kept drifting off. Back-to-back nights of guard duty were proving too much for him. Logan paced the room for a while, then sat on the floor. It wasn't very comfortable, so he hoped that would keep him awake.

Logan's chin slowly fell to his chest. Soon he heard a scraping at the window. *Stupid tree branch,* he thought sleepily. Then he noticed a cool breeze on his face. *That feels nice. Wait . . .*

He jerked awake. The window stood ajar, curtains fluttering.

Logan looked toward Gabby, and his mind exploded.

Two snatchers balanced easily on the sides of the crib like nightmarish chimpanzees. One reached for Gabby with its long, hairy arms.

Leaping up with a strangled cry, Logan rushed forward. The snatchers turned toward him with expressions of such menace that he nearly stumbled. But he was *not* going to let them take his cousin.

Logan dove toward Gabby. With a fierce hiss, the nearest snatcher backhanded him across the face. His head twisted painfully to one side, and he felt his neck pop. He staggered and fell to the floor. Before he could recover, the other snatcher scooped Gabby up, and both creatures leaped out the window.

Logan scrambled to his feet and rushed to the opening. Gabby's muffled cries floated on the warm night air. He launched himself through the window and landed hard on the decorative rocks below. Ignoring the pain in his hands and knees, he sprang up and raced after Gabby.

The snatchers had already disappeared into the pitch-black woods along the backyard. Logan reached the trees and recklessly plunged in. Moments later, he smacked his head on an unseen branch, and his legs flew out from under him. He slammed onto his back.

Logan sat up with a groan, gingerly fingering the lump on his forehead, and strained to catch a glimpse of the fleeing creatures. They were impossible to see in the nighttime woods, and Gabby's cries had already faded away. He scrambled to turn on his phone's flashlight, but his pocket was empty. His phone lay forgotten on the nursery floor.

Logan tugged fistfuls of his hair and choked out an ugly sob. Lurching to his feet, he pushed his way toward the house to wake Aunt Roslyn.

In the yard, he paused. Logan pictured himself telling his aunt he'd seen Gabby taken by two monsters. She wouldn't believe him, thinking he'd mistaken a human kidnapper in the darkness. She'd call the police, then force him to wait and tell them what happened. They wouldn't believe him either, and might take him to the precinct to work with a sketch artist like he'd seen on TV. That could take hours. Hours Gabby didn't have.

It was up to Logan to save her.

He clutched his head in both hands as the realization sank in. His mind revolted in fear and frustration. *I'm just a kid! This is too much for me! It isn't fair!*

But that didn't change anything, he realized. Kid or not, this was his fight.

He closed his eyes and took several deep, trembling breaths.

When he opened them, he knew what he had to do.

Logan ran onto the deck and tugged at the back door. Locked, like all the other doors. Running to the open nursery window, he jumped up and caught the ledge. Scrambling his feet against the wall, he pulled himself inside and fell to the carpet with a soft thump.

As Logan pushed himself up, he felt something gritty on his hands. A fine white powder stuck to his palms. Salt. He glanced back at the windowsill. Only a few scattered grains remained. The thick line he'd poured was gone. He examined the floor. Nothing. Aunt Roslyn must have found the salt during the day and thrown it out. He'd forgotten to check. Tears streamed down his face as a tsunami of guilt crashed over him.

He'd failed Gabby. It was his job to protect her, and now she'd been taken by monsters. He would never see her again. No one would. Aunt Roslyn would be devastated, and it was all his fault. Teo would be so disappointed in him.

As these horrible thoughts threatened to sweep him away, Logan focused on Gabby. He was the only one who knew the danger she was in. His jaws tightened. Something hardened inside of him, turning his guilt and grief to stone. Those feelings could wait. Gabby needed him, and he wouldn't fail her again.

Slipping into the guest room, Logan checked the windowsill. The salt was still there, so Meg would be safe—he hoped. He grabbed his backpack and some clothes and put them on in the hallway. In the kitchen, he took a flashlight from the junk drawer and put the large salt container in the backpack. Then he went to the garage and dug through a cabinet of sports equipment until he found a baseball bat.

Logan left the garage and raced through the night. Taking shortcuts through backyards and awkwardly jumping fences, he soon reached his destination and tapped lightly on a window.

A few moments later, Teo's sleepy face appeared. Her eyes widened in surprise, and she slid open the window.

"Logan, what are you—"

"There were two of them, and they took Gabby!" he said impatiently, then gave her a grim look. "We have to go to the cave."

CHAPTER 36

FIVE MINUTES later, Logan and Teo were
hurrying through the woods, chasing the jolting
beams of their flashlights. It was slow going. Navi-
gating the forest was infinitely more confusing in
the dark.

After half an hour of desperate searching, they finally found the eerie section of woods. Scratched and
breathing heavily, they stared uneasily at the warped
wall of trees. Already creepy in daylight, it was absolutely terrifying at night. The blood drained from

Logan's face, and his legs felt like soft butter. He tried to step forward, but his stomach roiled, and he nearly threw up. *I can't do this!*

Logan could feel his normal timid self battling desperately against his newfound courageous self. There had to be a way to fight back.

"Why do they do it?" he blurted out.

"What are you talking about?" Teo asked.

"The snatchers. Why do they kidnap babies?"

In the pale glow of their flashlights, Teo's face fell. She stared at the ground. "Um . . . I'm not sure."

"But you know something," he pressed. "Tell me."

Teo pulled her lower lip between her teeth. "I did come across some stuff during my research. There are different theories on why they do it, but no one seems to know for sure."

"So what are the theories?"

"Some think it's to punish humans who encroach on their territory."

Logan shook his head. "That doesn't make sense. The town has been here for a hundred years or something. They're the ones who just showed up."

Teo nodded. "Others say they raise the babies to work for them."

"That's a lot of time and effort to make a servant. What else?"

"Some believe the snatchers take them for . . ." She hesitated and looked away.

"For what?" Logan demanded.

Teo leveled her gaze at him. "For food."

He felt like he'd been gut punched by a giant. For a moment, Logan swayed unsteadily. Then, with a growl from deep in his throat, he surged forward.

It was like plunging into a black pool. The darkness almost smothered their flashlight beams, while the stifling trees thrust away the moonlight. Twisted roots seemed to rise up to trip them as they blundered through the underbrush. Logan jerked his head at every sound, certain it was a snatcher coming to attack. His blood pounded like a kick drum in his ears. Brandishing a field hockey stick she'd grabbed from her closet, Teo labored beside him, her face grim.

After forcing their way through yet another line of brush, they stumbled into an open space.

"Look familiar?" Logan whispered as he struggled to catch his breath.

Teo nodded, her flashlight trained on the tree she'd clung to while being dragged by the snatcher. "Pretty hard to forget."

They crossed the clearing, then pushed through the bushes until they reached Falcon Ridge. The cave opening loomed like a gaping maw, ready to swallow anyone foolish enough to enter.

"I can't believe we have to do this," Logan said in a choked voice. "I mean, *I* have to. She's my cousin, and I'm the one that screwed up. You could wait here."

Teo shot him a scornful look. "Like I'd let you go

in there alone. What kind of friend do you think I am? Besides, you'd never let me hear the end of it."

Logan gave her a grateful look as relief washed over him. "I was counting on you saying that. I just wanted credit for offering."

Drawing what felt like their final breaths, they knelt down and crawled into the cave.

CHAPTER 37

IT WAS the most terrifying thing Logan had ever done.

He trembled as they slowly advanced, the rocky ground cutting into his knees. The damp, low tunnel twisted and turned, hiding what lay ahead. Giant spiders, wriggling centipedes, and creepy-crawlies of every imaginable type scuttled in and out of their flashlight beams. Sticky webs clung to Logan's face and tangled in his hair. Every fiber of him screamed to turn back, to run, to forget he'd ever heard of missing babies and huddle in his safe, warm bed.

Teo was grimly silent, pushing the field hockey stick ahead of her. Her mouth was fixed in a firm line, and a frightened but stony look gleamed in her eyes.

She paused. After a moment, she pointed first to her ear, then into the darkness ahead of them.

Logan turned his head to listen down the tunnel. At first, he only heard the thunder of his heartbeat. Then there was something else.

The unmistakable cry of a baby.

Logan looked at Teo, his eyes wide. She pointed down at their flashlights, and he gave a reluctant nod. With twin clicks, they shut them off.

Logan had thought he'd known what darkness was, but on hands and knees in that spider-infested tunnel, with an eerie forest behind him and a pair of monsters ahead, he experienced true darkness for the first time. It was like someone had duct-taped his eyes and put a thick bag over his head. The blackness smothered him like a blanket, heavy and suffocating. He couldn't move.

Logan heard the scrape of Teo's hockey stick as she resumed crawling. As terrified as he was of going forward, being left alone was unbearable. Dragging one reluctant limb after another, he kept going.

The on-and-off cries of the baby echoed down the rocky tunnel, never seeming to come any closer. Logan listened intently. Was that Gabby? Was there more than one baby crying? He couldn't be sure.

They blindly felt their way along, sometimes painfully banging their heads on dips in the ceiling. After endless minutes, Logan thought he saw a pale glow in the distance. It was so faint, he wondered if he was imagining it. Then Teo gripped his arm—she'd seen it too.

They soon came to a dim shaft of light. It shone on the wall, near a bend in the tunnel. The baby's cries sounded close. Logan caught another sound now, something odd that he couldn't identify.

Teo's face was barely visible, but Logan read the

question in her eyes: *Are you ready?* He hesitated for a moment, then thought, *That really doesn't matter, does it?* He took a deep breath and nodded. They edged forward and peered around the bend. Logan's whole body went rigid as his brain screamed a single word—

No!

CHAPTER 38

LOGAN AND Teo gazed into a large rocky chamber. Bright moonlight poured in through a gap in the high ceiling, revealing natural ledges in the walls. Stalactites hung like giant stone icicles, their slick surfaces glistening faintly. The cave floor was dotted with shallow pools, occasionally disturbed by drips of water from above.

The five missing babies lay wrapped in blankets on the ground in the center of the chamber. And surrounding them, moving closer, were the snatchers.

Six snatchers.

Logan swayed unsteadily as the blood drained from his head. Seeing so many of these creatures, with their pointed muzzles, shaggy black hair, and glowing green eyes, was horrifying. It felt like a python was crushing his chest, and he gasped for breath. Splotches of light swam in his vision.

Then Logan's eyes landed on a blue blanket covered in ponies. There was Gabby, his helpless baby cousin whom he'd failed to protect. The one he'd already faced dark terrors to find. Whatever the consequences, he had to go on. He had to save her.

Gabby's plaintive cry echoed through the chamber. She sounded so vulnerable, so innocent, so helpless. A sudden rush of anger swept through Logan, burning away his paralyzing fear. A snatcher reached its clawed hand toward a baby. Logan felt Teo tense as they both prepared to rush forward.

Then another snatcher smacked the reaching hand

away. The offended creature gave a sharp hiss, and the two of them squared off against each other. The four remaining snatchers scurried toward the babies, their long arms outstretched. Noticing the movement, the first two snatchers broke apart and jumped toward their companions, pushing and scratching at them. Soon all six were shoving and hissing, each trying to get close to a baby.

One snatcher broke free of the tussle and grabbed a child, then raced to the far side of the cavern. The remaining snatchers stopped fighting, and each rushed to pick up a baby. When the furious scramble was over, five of the snatchers held babies while the sixth scuttled between them, screeching and trying to pull an infant from their arms. The snatchers holding the babies pushed their desperate companion away, cradling the babies gently and making creepy cooing noises.

Logan's jaw hung open. *What is going on?*

As he stared in amazement, he realized what was happening.

"They're *playing* with them," he said in a harsh whisper. "They're keeping the babies like *pets*!"

Teo grimaced. "But why are they fighting?"

Logan watched the six creatures continue to squabble over the five babies. Then he sucked in a breath. "They each want their own baby." His stomach clenched as he turned toward Teo. "To *keep*."

CHAPTER 39

"OH, THAT'S just not right," Teo muttered. She hefted her hockey stick and started forward.

Logan grabbed her arm. "Wait." Taking the salt container from his backpack, he spread a thick line along the ground where the tunnel opening met the cavern. Returning the container to his pack, he tightened his grip on the baseball bat and nodded to Teo.

Leaping up with wild cries, they clicked on their flashlights and burst into the chamber.

The distracted snatchers were caught completely off guard. They stumbled backward with loud shrieks, clutching the babies protectively to their chests. Teo and Logan pressed their advantage, pushing forward with their weapons outstretched.

Moments later, they stood before the snatchers as the creatures crouched with their backs against the far wall. Logan and Teo set their flashlights on the ground to free both hands for fighting.

"Give me my cousin!" Logan yelled, brandishing his bat in what he hoped was a menacing way.

"Yeah, drop those babies!" Teo shouted. "But, you know, carefully!"

Recovering quickly from the surprise attack, the snatchers hissed loudly at Logan and Teo, their faces pulled into horrifying expressions. They were no longer startled. They were furious.

With a blood-chilling cry, the snatcher without a baby launched itself at Teo with its claws outstretched. She swung her hockey stick, knocking the creature toward Logan. He slammed his bat into its shoulder and sent it tumbling across the floor.

The kids turned to face the five remaining snatchers, then hesitated. Each creature held an infant. How could Logan and Teo attack them without hurting a baby?

Sensing the kids' indecision, the snatchers moved forward. One leaped close with blurring speed and swiped at Logan's leg. He howled in pain as its claws sliced through his jeans, leaving parallel cuts on his calf. As Teo turned to help, another snatcher darted in and slashed her above the waist. She gasped in shock and whirled around again.

The snatchers quickly surrounded them. Logan and Teo instinctively stood back-to-back, spinning slowly with their weapons outstretched. Whichever snatchers they weren't facing dashed in to strike at their arms and legs.

A sickening realization settled in Logan's stomach like a block of ice—he didn't think they could save the babies.

He wasn't even sure they could save themselves.

CHAPTER 40

THE RING of snatchers slowly tightened around Logan and Teo. Their emerald eyes burned with hatred as they hissed and snapped their jaws.

Teo lunged toward the nearest creature. Swinging her hockey stick in a high arc, she smacked it down on top of the snatcher's skull. There was a sharp crack, and the creature staggered back, howling in pain. Logan and Teo scrambled through the break in the circle. Teo accidentally kicked a flashlight, sending its beam spinning wildly. Reaching the cave wall, they turned to face the creatures in a defensive crouch.

The snatchers regrouped and came slowly toward them in a line. The one Teo had struck walked unsteadily, like it was still dazed. Taking a cue from her successful attack, Logan jumped forward and swung his bat down at the nearest snatcher's head.

The bat slammed to a stop in midair, inches above its target. With incredible speed and strength, the snatcher had caught the bat in one hand while protectively cradling a crying Gabby in the other. It gave the weapon a sudden jerk, yanking the bat from Logan's grip and pulling him off-balance. He fell into a shallow pool on the cave floor as the snatcher tossed the bat aside and closed in. Logan scuttled away like a crab until he reached the opposite chamber wall. Nowhere left to run.

Teo desperately tried to reach him, but she was pinned by the others, who now nimbly avoided her skull strikes. She swung her stick at the nearest snatcher's legs, but the creature was too fast. It leaped over the slashing stick like a jump rope.

"If I try anything else, I'll hit the babies!" Teo cried. "What do we do?"

"You're asking *me*?" Weaponless, Logan kicked out at the approaching snatcher. It caught his foot and began pulling him closer. He gripped an outcropping of rock with both hands, suddenly locked in a deadly tug-of-war. With a desperate twist of his leg, Logan's shoe came off in the snatcher's hand. The creature fell onto its back, cradling Gabby to its chest.

The snatcher without a baby turned from attacking Teo and raced over to its fallen companion. Instead of helping the snatcher up, it grabbed Gabby from the creature's arms. With a gleeful cackle, the snatcher hugged her close and raced toward the tunnel. It was abandoning the fight and leaving with its prize.

"No!" Logan screamed, his arm outstretched

helplessly toward the fleeing monster. It was taking Gabby, and he was too far away to stop it. There was no telling where the snatcher would go.

Gabby gave a pitiful wail, and Logan's heart shattered. She would disappear again—this time, forever.

CHAPTER 41

WHEN THE escaping snatcher reached the tunnel, there was a sudden flash of flames. The creature staggered back, howling in pain. Smoke rose from its foot, and the cave filled with the noxious odor of burning hair.

"The salt!" Teo cried, still fending off the other snatchers. "It worked!"

Gripped by sudden inspiration, Logan tore off his backpack and pulled out the salt container. Scooping a quick handful, he threw it at the snatcher in front of him.

The creature screamed in agony. Smoke billowed up in nauseating waves as the snatcher clawed at its chest. Logan flung another handful, bigger this time. Now the creature danced in pain, its high-pitched shrieks echoing wildly in the enclosed space.

The other snatchers paused and stared at their companion in confusion. Logan grabbed a huge handful of salt, then replaced the lid. "Catch!" he yelled, and threw Teo the container.

Teo caught it and pried off the lid. Taking a handful, she swept the salt over the snatchers in front of her. They howled and fell writhing to the ground.

His eyes smoldering, Logan bore down on the snatcher holding Gabby and menacingly shook his fistful of salt. The creature backed away, hissing while clutching Gabby to its chest. Logan trapped it in a corner of the cave. Then, before it could dart away, he poured the salt over its head.

The snatcher shrieked, and its eyes went wide. As it

grew limp, Logan grabbed Gabby from its unresisting arms. Its long black hair shriveled away to nothing. The snatcher stood like a misshapen, naked chimp. Then the creature's flesh melted away like snow before Logan's horrified eyes. Soon there was only a skeleton, which collapsed in a clattering heap. Finally, even the bones crumbled to gray powder.

Teo continued throwing salt on the remaining snatchers. Racing to help, Logan dashed among them, catching babies as they fell from the creatures' arms.

Moments later, the only sound in the cave was the ragged breathing of two exhausted kids and the wailing of five babies. Logan gently cradled Gabby and another child as he looked wearily around the chamber.

There was nothing left of the snatchers but six piles of ash.

CHAPTER 42

LOGAN GRIMACED as the paramedic tight-ened a bandage around his leg.

"Take it easy for a while," she said. "And don't get this wet."

"Don't worry, he never showers anyway," Teo said.

The paramedic smiled, then gave Logan a quizzical look. "Are you sure you got those cuts from thorns? They're pretty deep . . . and unusually parallel."

"Yep," Logan said with a forced smile. "They were *big* thorns."

The paramedic nodded doubtfully. She walked away, leaving Teo and Logan in the back of the ambulance. It was the first time they'd been alone since they'd emerged from the woods with the babies and called the police.

"Think everyone's buying our story?" Teo asked quietly.

Logan yawned loudly and gazed out the open ambulance doors at the purple sunrise peeking over the trees. While police kept the media and onlookers away, Aunt Roslyn stood clutching Gabby, alongside the Dankworths and three other couples. They were all crying and holding their babies close while casting grateful glances at Logan and Teo.

"What's to doubt?" he asked. "We told them the only story they'd believe."

The police had arrived within minutes of their call. Logan and Teo told them they'd dared each other to sneak into the woods that night and had discovered the babies alone in a cave. Some of the police took charge of the infants, while others had Teo and Logan lead them to the cave to try and catch the kidnappers. They'd played along, knowing there was nothing to find but ash and scattered salt.

"Do you think we should have told them the truth?"

Logan shook his head. "We talked about this. Without the bodies of the snatchers, how could we prove it? They'd think we were lying or having the same issues as Elena."

"But people will still worry, thinking the kidnapper got away."

"I know, but things will calm down when everyone realizes the kidnappings have stopped."

"True," Teo said, and then her face broke into a grin. "And in the meantime, I guess we'll just have to get used to being heroes."

Logan gave a tired laugh. "My parents come home today. I'll settle for not being grounded."

Teo looked thoughtful. "One thing I can't figure out—the babies seemed pretty healthy. How did the snatchers feed them?" She wrinkled her nose. "You don't think they, you know, nursed—"

"Stop right there," Logan said, looking uncomfortable. "There are some things I don't want to know."

CHAPTER 43

One week later . . .

MOONLIGHT SHONE through the curtains of Meg's bedroom, tracing eerie shapes on the carpet. The house was deathly still, as if under a spell.

The deep silence was broken by a soft scratching at the window.

Meg stirred in her bed. As the sound continued, she forced herself awake and sat up groggily.

Her gaze fell on the curtains.

Moving slowly, Meg got up and tiptoed across the room. When she reached the window, the scratching stopped. She stood trembling for a long moment. Then she grasped the curtains and pulled them aside.

Meg gasped in shock.

On the other side of the glass perched a hideous form, like a misshapen monkey with a sharp muzzle. It regarded her with emerald eyes.

"Ollie!" she cried softly.

Meg quickly opened the window, then stepped back as the creature slipped through and dropped to the floor.

"I'm so glad you're okay!" Meg said as she wrapped the creature in a tight hug. "I was *so* worried about you. I tried to lead my annoying big brother away from your cave that day, but he just wouldn't give up!" She scowled angrily in the direction of Logan's bedroom. "I'm sorry about your family, but don't worry. I won't let him hurt you."

The snatcher purred as she scratched its head and stroked the long fur on its back.

"So," Meg said with a sly grin, "are you ready to get me another baby to play with?"

ACKNOWLEDGMENTS

HAVING AN artistic family rocks. Life would not be nearly as fun without the creative synergy I have with my author wife, Lisa; artist son, Kilian; and actor daughter, Kennedy. I love you all.

Thanks to Mom and Dad for a lifetime of unwavering support and to Holli and Shannon for always looking out for your little brother. Casey, Chloe, Jackson, and Lily, thanks for letting me hang out with you.

Michael Bourret, you are a wildly wonderful combination of supportive and honest, smart and snarky, insightful and hilarious. You're going to have to pry me off your client list with a crowbar.

Stephanie Pitts, you're the best editor an author could hope for. The fact that you're my first editor doesn't take away from your unquestionable awesomeness or keep you from being my favorite.

Matt Phipps, your positive attitude, kindness, and professionalism shine through in everything you do. I'm lucky to have your input on my books and career.

Ryan Quickfall, these books would not be what they are without your incredibly spooky, eye-catching cover illustrations. I'm so glad we get to scare kids together.

A jumbo-sized thanks to publisher and friend Jen Klonsky, cover designer Danielle Ceccolini, copyeditors Ana Deboo and Cindy Howle, and everyone at Penguin Young Readers, including art, sales, marketing, publicity, and school and library. I couldn't be on a better team.

This book would never find its way into readers' hands without the tireless efforts of booksellers, librarians, and teachers. To all of you, my deep and sincere thanks for the work you do and for how you've embraced me and the Monsterious series. I'm honored to partner with you to help kids fall in love with reading.

A special shout-out to Melissa Thom, Carrie Seiden, Jennifer Halbur, Cindy Schwind, and the rest of the #BookPosse for all the tweets and support!

Finally, to you, my wonderful readers: Without you, the monsters in these pages would only be haunting my dreams. Thanks for coming on this wild ride with me. Here's to more spooky adventures together!

Photo © Kennedy McMann

As a professional musician, **Matt McMann** played an NFL stadium, a cruise ship, and the International Twins Convention. Now he writes the kind of spooky mystery-adventure books he loved as a kid. He's hiked the Pacific Northwest, cruised Loch Ness, and chased a ghost on a mountain. While he missed Bigfoot and Nessie, he caught the ghost. He enjoys brainstorming new books with his wife, *New York Times* bestselling author Lisa McMann; viewing his son Kilian McMann's artwork; and watching his daughter, actor Kennedy McMann, on television.

You can visit Matt at
MattMcMann.com

And follow him on Instagram and Twitter
@Matt_McMann